IRISH CROSSINGS

DANNY'S STORY

TERENCE O'LEARY

Also by Terence O'Leary

Irish Crossings - Caitlin & Paddy's Story
Bringing Boomer Home
Penalty Kick
More Than a Game

Swan
Creek
Press

Copyright 2017 Terence O'Leary
All rights reserved
First Swan Creek Press, LLC Edition 2018
ISBN: 0975321692
ISBN 13: 9780975321690
Library of Congress Control Number: 2018901634
Swan Creek Press, Toledo, OH

www.terenceoleary.com

In Memory of
Patrick and Catherine Feeney

They led their children out of Ireland during the time of the
Great Hunger. They didn't survive the voyage to America, but
their son, my Grandfather's Grandfather, lived to tell their
story.

For my Friend
Dennis Bova

"It is in the shelter of each other that people live."
-an ancient Irish proverb

Caitlin stopped and stood with the basket of flowers. She lovingly gazed at her Gigi. Her Great-Grandmother had lived nearly a century. She was the last living link to Caitlin's Irish ancestors who came to America. The frail woman sat in a wheelchair in the shade of a linden tree in the small garden behind the nursing home. A white shawl covered her sparse grey hair and rested on her shoulders. Arthritis had turned her back into a widow's hump and gnarled her fingers. The wind stirred and tree blossoms floated gently down upon her.

Caitlin quietly approached so as not to startle her. With her head bent down, the old woman first saw the basket of flowers. She gently caressed the petals of the white Easter lilies. She strained to tilt her head up. When she saw Caitlin, she smiled.

Caitlin set the small woven basket onto Gigi's lap and kissed her forehead. Gigi's fingers found and entwined the young woman's long, red hair. Gigi sighed in contentment and then pointed to the wrought iron bench. Caitlin wheeled her Great-Grandmother forward and sat so they were facing.

"How have you been?" Caitlin asked.

Gigi pondered the question and then said, "All the days seem the same here." She fingered the white petals. "Is it Easter?"

Caitlin shook her head and said, "No. I was at the shop and these flowers seemed to call out to me."

"Irish Easter lilies. When I was young, men would wear them on their lapels to honor the fallen Irish patriots." She grew pensive.

Caitlin waited. She knew her Great-Grandmother's many moods. She would talk when she was ready.

"I never met Danny. My Gigi," she looked at the teenager, "my Grandmother, who you were named after, said she only saw him once. Caitlin and her husband Paddy left at the beginning of the Great Hunger. They left their brothers and sisters behind. Danny came later.

She smelled the flowers that rested on her lap. "My Grandmother said he didn't stay long, only long enough to tell his story."

IRELAND 1847
THE GREAT
HUNGER

CHAPTER 1

I do not know why I lived while so many died.

I wiped my tears on my coat sleeve. Paddy and Caitlin were going to America and I didn't know if I'd ever see them again. We left them on the ship. I turned back at the end of the wharf and raised my hand for a final wave, but they were already gone into the hold of the wooden sailing ship. My Da took my arm and pulled me along. I cried for the loss of the parting, but also because I knew my whole life had suddenly changed. Paddy was the oldest in our family and with him now gone, I carried a terrible burden. I was the oldest son.

We walked through the city. Thick billowing, dark clouds rolled in like waves from the sea and brought a hard rain. The street was crowded with Irish, mostly men who were common laborers. They carried their few possessions on their backs. They didn't have the money to go to America, but those who had a few shillings could ride with the livestock on the ferry boats that crossed the Irish Sea to England. The lucky would find work in English fields. At least in England, if no work was to be found, they wouldn't starve. We learned early that the Queen feeds her subjects in England, but not in Ireland. We were to fend for ourselves.

Food brought the starving Irish to the city. They followed the grain carts and livestock from the fields to the ports. There was food aplenty in the shops for those with coins in their pockets. But the poor had no coins and there was no manna falling from heaven. Those who couldn't pay their fares to England were left to beg. Families wearing all they possessed huddled out of the rain in the lee of the buildings. I felt their eyes as we passed. I wondered what would become of them.

My Da trudged through the muddy streets seeming oblivious to his surroundings. The rain wouldn't slow him. I turned my collar up and titled my cap over my eyes and followed in his footsteps. He set a strong, fast pace. I had to struggle to keep up with his longer stride.

When I couldn't bear his fast pace any longer, I shouted, "I'm tired, Da."

He kept walking. I fought to keep up as the path steepened in the green hills. My foot stumbled on a rock. My legs buckled and I fell to the ground. The rain had stopped, but the path was still wet. Mud sank into my trousers.

He stopped, then came and towered over me. "You're not Paddy, that's for sure. Come on, get up. They'll be no moon tonight. We'll not find our way back in the dark." He grabbed the back of my coat and yanked me to my feet.

"I'm hungry."

"I'm sure your Ma has scrounged up something for us at home." He roughly clutched my upper arm and pulled me with him. "It's not that much farther. Paddy and I would have been home by now."

I snapped, "I'm not, Paddy."

"There's no time for you to be a child. If we're going to survive, you must be a man."

He released my arm and walked ahead of me in the fading light. I had no choice but to follow.

As it grew darker, I wanted to hold his hand. I've always been afraid to be outside in the dark. When it is cloudy with no moon, the darkness swallows you. I could feel the banshees and pookas circling, coming closer and closer. I knew they'd snatch me from behind and my Da would never find me in the dark. I followed my Da's breathing and his light footsteps on the path. When he started to vanish in the blackness, I ran forward and grabbed the back of his coat with my shaking hands. He didn't seem to mind. We kept climbing. I knew we reached the top of the hill when I felt the cold wind.

I saw the light and wanted to run the rest of the way home. My sisters had made a fire outside our cottage's doorway. We followed the beacon to the cottage. My brother, Michael, sat by the fire and watched for us. He jumped in fright when we stepped out of the darkness. My father laughed, ruffled Michael's hair, then walked into the cottage.

I followed him inside the warm room and collapsed at the table. I was exhausted, way beyond hungry. I don't know how many miles we walked today. All I wanted to do was sleep. I laid my head on my forearm and watched my Ma stir the kettle above the peat fire. Smoke rose from the hearth and drifted into the thatched roof. My Ma set a wooden bowl of soup in front of Da. My oldest sister, Mary, slid a bowl in front of me. My Da stirred his spoon in the bowl and then lifted it. The potatoes had been long gone. He searched for any hidden morsels and was lucky to find bits of turnips. He slurped loudly.

I finished and Mary filled me another bowl. The soup was warm and eased the cravings in my stomach. But I knew I'd pay the price. I already felt my bowels loosening.

CHAPTER 2

Shouts awoke me. If the cow could run, she would. But she was trapped in the cottage. I had taken Paddy's place watching over our livestock, Millie and our pig. I slept in front of the hearth in the small cottage originally built for my Ma and Da. When us kids came along they needed more room, so they built our larger home and left this for the animals.

Coghlan burst through the doorway with a club in his fist. He was a man to instill fear in any child. He was Lord Townsend's agent and controlled our destiny. I was paralyzed with fright. I cowered on my straw mat on the ground. My Da rushed in and stood between me and the Devil.

"Gale Day has come and gone," Coghlan said. "You have no money to pay the rent." He pointed the club at Millie. "We'll take the cow."

"You can't," my Da said.

"Then pay what's due."

My father's shoulders slumped. "I can't," he said resignedly. "Take the pig instead."

"We have plenty of pigs. It's the cow I want."

"For God's sake take the pig and leave me my cow."

Coghlan smashed the club against the stone rock in front of the hearth. "Your cow or your cottage. You choose."

The pig squealed. Millie snorted, shook her head and swished her tail. The bell she wore clanged. I ran and stood by my Da's side. Two more men came in. One of them carried a rope.

"That's no way to do this," my Da shouted above the squealing and Millie's bellowing. I could feel his anger. "Go. Wait outside. I'll bring her to you."

Coghlan motioned to his men and they all left.

I was glad Paddy wasn't here. I don't know what he would have done. He raised Millie since she was a calf. She quieted when the strangers left. My Da sang softly as he slowly approached her. He ran his hands gently over her flank.

"'I hope you give sour milk for a month. It'll serve them right." He slipped our rope around her neck and led her to the door.

My Ma and two sisters and young Michael stood in the doorway of our cottage. Michael snuck out from behind them. He ran and joined me.

"What are they doing?" he asked.

"They're taking Millie."

My Da gave the rope to Coghlan. Then he untied Millie's bell and held it at his side.

"We'll go to Cornelius Donavan's next," Coghlan said.

He passed the rope to the tallest of his men. Millie fought them. She snorted and shook her head. One man pulled the rope as the other smacked her hide. I saw fright in Millie's eyes. The spell came over me. I rushed the man hitting Millie and tried to knock him to the ground. He spun and backhanded me. His knuckles felt like a rock. I fell and my jaw throbbed. I struggled to my feet to charge again.

My Da shouted, "Danny."

He ran and snatched my collar. He yanked me back and wrapped me in his arms. I hit him with my elbows trying to break free. He just held me tighter.

"You got what you came for. Now go!" my Da shouted at Coghlan.

I was seething. It was like a fire burned within me that I couldn't put out.

Coghlan came forward. He bounced the club against his open palm. His black beard was stained with tobacco juice. The breeze carried his whiskey odor. He stared at me like I was some sort of animal.

My Da said, "Just go and leave us be."

Coghlan's eyes left mine and went to my Da's. "Your potatoes are gone. Your days are numbered." He laughed. He pointed to our rotten potato fields. "This will all be pasture. The cow will live longer than you."

Silence followed his words. Millie quieted. Coghlan turned and waved his hand at his men. They led our cow away. When they reached the crossroad, my Da's arms relaxed. The fight had left me. I felt hollow and helpless.

Michael picked up Millie's bell that my Da had dropped. He carried it and offered it to my Da, but he just shook his head. He turned away from us and walked out to the barren fields.

CHAPTER 3

It had only been six weeks since Caitlin and Paddy's wedding. But it had been a month without potatoes. I couldn't believe how much our lives had changed. Before, I was never hungry. Now, I always was. Before, we may not have had meat, but we always had potatoes. Even in the hungry months there were always some potatoes left. Now, we had soup three times a day. There were days when the soup tasted like boiled water. Soup never filled me like potatoes. I was always hungry. I wondered if I would stop growing.

With Paddy gone, I tried to find my new place in our family. Mary was 15 and the eldest and Joanna next at 14. I was 10 and the oldest boy. Michael was only 8.

When I was younger, my sisters seemed to spend all their time with my Ma. They'd cook and sew. When we had Millie, they'd churn the milk for butter. Mary and Joanna had their own bed and at night, I would hear them talking and giggling. For the most part they ignored me. They doted on Michael. He was the baby and could do no wrong.

Now, my sisters spent their days searching the fields for food with my Ma. Fall was turning into winter. They dug for roots. Turnips were prized. Each day became more of a struggle as the picking grew slimmer. They'd take Michael with them. They left me to watch over our cottage and our pig.

Our nights were quiet. Our house became as somber as a church.

Before the blight, my Da spent his days working the fields. Now, he would leave early in the morning and walk west to Skibbereen or east to Rosscarbery. He searched for any labor that would pay a few coins for a bag of grain or a loaf of bread. Most nights he returned with nothing but a grim look on his haggard, bearded face. I asked to go with him, but he said I would just slow him down.

CHAPTER 4

Joanna would call me for breakfast. If she had to call me more than once, she'd send Michael to rouse me from my bed. Soon as she saw me stand, our pig would start to squeal. I think she missed the potatoes more than I did. It was getting harder and harder to feed her. There weren't any table scraps for us, so of course there were none for her. I wondered if that was why my Da wanted to keep Millie. Our cow could feed herself off the grass on the hillside and give us milk for free.

One morning before he left to search for work my Da came into the cottage. I started to get up, hoping that he would take me with him, but he just waved me down. He stood over our pig, then crouched down to her level. He rubbed her ears and felt her sides. The saddest look came over his face. He stood and without a look my way, he walked from the cottage. I knew I wouldn't see him until nighttime.

I went and crouched the way my Da did. The pig's snout searched my hand for food. I felt her sides. I could feel her ribs. I don't know where the thought came from, but with it came a sudden pain in my stomach. If we couldn't feed her she would waste away to nothing. The pain spread when I realized we couldn't let that happen. I fell away from her. She came forward, her snout seeking. I pushed her away with my foot. I scampered back and stood. She squealed.

Suddenly, I was crying. I said to her, "We have no choice. If we can't feed you then you must feed us while you still can." I ran from the cottage. I stopped and wiped the tears from my cheeks. I walked back and closed the bottom of the cottage door.

Our pig stared up at me. I knew what had to be done. What I didn't know was why my Da wasn't doing it.

CHAPTER 5

I sat on the grass still wet with morning dew. From where I sat, I could still see our cottage. I watched to make sure no one came for our pig. It was one of our few cloudless days. The sun woke up the land. As the grass dried it seemed to grow in front of my eyes. I pulled a piece of grass and munched on the stem to try and sooth my stomach's hunger.

I sat where Paddy sat the day before he left. His dream was to build a cottage on this highest piece of land. To farm the land and share his life with Caitlin and the children he hoped would come. But the blight came and our lives changed. My Da sent Paddy to America and Caitlin went with him. Now, they were both gone to America, never to return.

With all the rain we had the grass was never greener. Coghlan was right. Cows would thrive in these fields. If we could live on grass we would thrive with them. But we weren't like Millie. Cows had grass and we had our potatoes, but all the potatoes were rotten. What I never understood was why only the potatoes were blighted. Everything else that came from the ground was fine. Carrots and turnips that grew in the same fields were healthy. In summer, strawberries were there for the picking. Lord Townsend's grain harvest was plentiful during all the years of famine.

I remembered my Da telling Paddy we couldn't grow grain to eat because we didn't have enough land. Potatoes grew thick and plentiful. On our small farm no other crop except potatoes would feed the family for the year. So year after year as long as I could remember it was potatoes that we grew. We came to depend on the one crop, but when the potatoes turned black we had nothing else to eat.

My Da said when he was younger there were times of famine, but only for a season. Last year we survived because only some of the potatoes were rotten. This year they were all ruined.

We must have food or surely we'd all die. From the top of the hill, my Ma and siblings looked like blackbirds hunched over in the field as their fingers clawed for roots.

I tried to think of what else we could do. We're not allowed to hunt on Lord Townsend's land or fish his streams. If caught, you would be sent to jail and maybe hanged. I pulled and chewed another stem of grass. The sun's rays cleared the top of the distant hills. Through the gaps between the hills, I could see the dab of blue beyond the valley. On the road leading to the sea, I watched carts of grain leave Lord Townsend's estate to travel to the port of Cobh, never to be seen by the likes of us again.

Chapter 6

My Da came home early, empty-handed as usual. My Ma and siblings were still in the fields. Dark clouds followed him. It would storm tonight. He sent me down the road to Caitlin's family's cottage. He told me to tell Caitlin's Da that we would butcher our pig tonight. Caitlin and Paddy's marriage joined our families together. Thomas was to bring his family, but to tell no one else.

The heavy downpour seemed to coincide with Thomas' entrance into our cottage. Sarah was right behind him with Brigid, whose hand seemed attached to her mother's skirt. Brigid was a child younger than Michael. I don't think she'd grown a smidgen since I last saw her. Mary and Joanna quickly enticed the young girl away from her mother.

My Da asked, "Where're the boys?"

Thomas shook water from his cap then set it back on his head. He went and stood by the hearth and the warmth of the fire. Steam rose off his clothes.

"I sent James and Dennis to stay with my brother in Cork. He owns a small pub down by the docks. He's family. They'll stay with him until they find jobs or until the potatoes come back." He shook his head. "When Coghlan took our last pig, he left me no choice." He spat into the fire. "God damn him." He smacked the table. "We have nothing left to eat." He heaved out a breath and then took in another. "At least the boys are safe. They won't starve under my brother's roof."

"You'll have some of the pig," my Da said.

"A blessing on you and your family."

The wind howled and torrents of rain beat the roof.

"We're all family here," my Da said.

Thomas nodded and said, "You've picked a good night."

"On a clear night, they'd smell the pig for miles. The rain will keep the smell inside. " My Da's face turned somber. "I know it's not right. They're our neighbors. We should share. But..."

He stared into the fire. He couldn't find the words to finish his thought.

We butchered the pig in the small cottage, but there wasn't much of a feast. We ate just a little, then cured and saved as much of the ham as we could. Even the pig's bone marrow would sweeten our soup. The taste of fresh bacon was a treat that I carried with me for days.

After the meal, Thomas shared some tobacco with my Da. They both sat by the fire while the women took the table.

"Do you think they're in America now?" Thomas asked.

"Seamus said it could take six weeks or more and that's if they had good weather," my Da replied.

"Caitlin promised her mother she'd write. But it'll be months before we get a letter."

"I didn't know Caitlin could write. None of my children can."

Thomas glanced at his wife. "Sarah learned her letters from the nuns when she was an orphan. She taught our children what she knew." He sighed and blew smoke at the fire. "It's the not knowing that keeps me up at night. Are they safe?" He stared at Joseph. "Did we do right by my Caitlin and your Paddy to send them away?"

"There's no life for them here, Thomas. At least in America, they have a chance, a chance for themselves and their children." The pipe embers flared as he sucked in the smoke. "The pig's gone. What savings we had went to pay for their crossing. Next time Coghlan comes for the rent there'll be nothing to give him. He'll throw us out and tumble my cottage. There's nothing I can do to stop him."

"Surely, you don't think Lord Townsend would let Coghlan do that?"

"Lord Townsend may not want to, but he will. If he can't get money from us, he'll get it from our land. The land my Grandfather's Grandfather farmed."

"There's no work in the towns?" Thomas asked.

Joseph shook his head. "No work, just rumors of work. They say the government will set some men to building roads."

"The British must do something. They take our grain and livestock. They must give us something in return."

"They'll give us nothing. They want us gone."

It was like a black cloud descended upon my Da. His face hardened and his eyes flashed anger. It was truly scary to behold.

CHAPTER 7

Our world turned cold. With the pig butchered, there was no livestock left to watch over, so I returned to the main cottage and my bed with Michael. I took to waking early in the morning. Most mornings, I would enjoy the warmth of our straw mattress and try to remember my dreams. Lying next to me, Michael would snore softly and give off heat that would rival the peat in our hearth.

My Da was always the first to get out of bed. He'd take no food or water. He'd put on his coat and cap and leave without a word or a glance to me. When he opened the door, cold air would rush in and I'd snuggle closer to my brother. I knew my Da wouldn't return until nighttime.

My Ma was up next. She'd boil pig bones in water and call it breakfast. They were the same bones she boiled the day before. The pig's meat was saved to be added to the soup for dinner.

I got out of bed and walked and sat at the table. I could still remember the days when my Ma would set a steaming bowl of potatoes before me. I'd take one and mash it in my bowl. My Ma liked to sing in the mornings. She'd tease me with a cup of buttermilk until I joined her singing and then she'd pour the buttermilk on top of my potatoes.

My Ma had stopped singing. I'd smile at her to try and get her to smile in return. Some days she would, but most days she wouldn't. She'd move slowly around the table to go and wake my sisters. Everything seemed to be such an effort for her.

The pig was gone and with him went my job to watch over him. My Da wouldn't take me with him because he said I'd slow him down. My Ma and siblings didn't need me to help search the same fields over and over again. The roots were harder and harder to find. I was on my own, so I took to wandering. I'd leave after breakfast. I searched for anything that we could eat.

We lived in Carrigillihy. If you were to walk south or east you'd find the ocean. To the east the ocean was just a finger that poked into the land. You could stand on one side and see land across the water on the other side. But unless you had a boat, there was no way to get across except for the long walk along the tip of the finger. To the south was the coast of Ireland where in wintertime thunderous waves would crash upon the shore.

We lived near the ocean, but in our hamlet, we were farmers, not fishermen. When I was little, I asked my Da why we didn't fish. He laughed and said it was because we couldn't swim.

My Da would leave when there was just enough light to see the road in front of our cottage. Many times he would take off and disappear into the morning fog. Not me. I'd wait until I was sure the sun had chased the banshees and leprechauns back to their homes before my feet would touch the path. With winter coming, each day was shorter than the last. I didn't want to be caught out in the dark. No matter where I roamed, when noontime came, I started for home.

It was cold in the mornings. I'd walk with my hands in my pockets and my coat's collar turned up around my neck. It was quiet in the countryside. Sometimes it was so quiet, I thought even the birds were afraid to sing.

The Hegartys' cottage was on the edge of our hamlet. Cornelius was about my age and we'd play in the churchyard after Mass, but neither Cor nor his family was at Sunday Mass for the last couple weeks. I stood and stared at their cottage from the road. No one was out in their fields. I wondered if they were one of the families who left without a word of goodbye. My curiosity got the better of me.

As I got closer, the cottage seemed deserted. It was enveloped by the terrible stink that came from the rotten potatoes. The cottage's door was shut. I stood outside and shouted, "Hello." No one answered. I walked up and pounded on the door. The wood rattled against the latch. I walked around the cottage and then stepped back and looked at the roof. There was no smoke, so I knew there was no peat fire in the hearth. I walked and shouted, "Hello" out to the fields, but only my words echoed back.

I convinced myself that they were gone. I knew they wouldn't leave any food behind, but maybe they left something that I could give to my Da to take and sell in exchange for grain. It took a while to build up my courage. I pounded and then rattled the door. I gave it a good kick, but the latch held. Now, I was mad. I slammed my shoulder harder and harder against the door. It gave and I fell into the room.

The smell made me gag. My eyes adjusted to the half-light from the doorway. I stared not understanding what I saw. I stood and walked closer. The family was in the corner lying on a straw mattress. I couldn't tell where one body stopped and another began. I inched closer. The only sound was my breathing. Cor was on the edge of the mattress. His eyes were open. His purple tongue hung out from the side of his mouth. I don't know if I screamed, but I do know I ran all the way home.

CHAPTER 8

The Hegartys' were the first of the many dead that I was to see. Cor's face still haunts me in my dreams.

When I got home, I blurted out my story so quickly that my Ma could barely understand what I said. She wouldn't do anything until my Da got home. I walked in circles in front of our cottage. I saw my Da down the end of our lane and ran to him. I told him my story and he took me with him.

The Hegartys' cottage door was still open. I wouldn't go in with my Da. He wasn't in the cottage long. He pulled the door shut behind him.

"There's nothing we can do tonight."

I didn't know if he said the words to me or himself.

"What happened, Da?"

He squeezed my shoulder. "Sometimes people just give up."

"How did they die?"

"They stopped trying, so they starved to death."

I said in a small voice, "We could have given them some of the pig."

He grabbed my jaw and turned my face up to him. "No. We couldn't. The pig was ours. We need his food to survive." He jabbed a finger at the cottage. "Are you going to be like them and give up?"

The anger came like lightning. I pushed his hand away and glared at him.

He smiled as if he saw something he wanted. He turned from me and looked at the cottage.

"It's too late for a wake. Their souls have long been gone. It'll be dark soon. There's no time to bury them now. I'll come back in the morning."

He pushed me toward the path to the road. He said from behind me, "Their door was open?"

I knew he knew the answer, so I shook my head.

"They barred the door to keep the banshees and animals away from them."

I waited for his next question, but he was silent the rest of the way home.

CHAPTER 9

My sisters said it wasn't right for Brigid to be all alone. They said every child needed brothers and sisters. Brigid's sister, Caitlin, left with my oldest brother, Paddy, for America. Brigid's brothers were staying in Cork with their uncle. Mary and Joanna set out to adopt Brigid and that's what they did.

Brigid was waif-like, younger, and smaller than Michael. She was a quiet girl, at least around me. Her cottage was the closest to ours and just a short walk down the lane. After breakfast the girls would go and gather her up. Her parents never seemed to mind. My sisters would keep an eye on her and Michael while they searched for roots.

The Hegartys' farm was deserted, so my Ma took her helpers to their fields. They'd stop at the Hegartys' graves and they'd all kneel and say a prayer for their souls before they began their search. For the first couple days, it was like they went to the market. They'd find turnips and carrots in the Hegartys' deserted fields.

My Da scavenged what he could from the Hegartys'. He carried their spades and picks and axes, iron pots and pans to Skibbereen. He'd return home with a bag of corn on his shoulder.

We headed into winter. There were days when the rains would come so cold and heavy that they'd drive everyone inside except for my Da. The girls would play. It was like my older sisters became children again. I still remember the first time I heard Brigid laugh. It was such a strange and wonderful sound in our cottage.

If the rain wouldn't stop, my sisters would keep Brigid for the night. She'd sleep between Mary and Joanna, with the two of them watching over her as if she was their own child.

CHAPTER 10

Winter had come and the fields were barren.

We didn't have potatoes, but we had plenty of peat. My Ma would keep the fire going day and night. We were always hungry that winter, but at least we were warm inside our cottage.

My Da finally found work and that is how we survived. The English needed men to build a road up around Catheragh. He didn't want to, but he took me with him. I was only a boy of 11. The English would pay an able-bodied boy half of a man's wages. We needed the money to buy food for the family.

We'd leave well before sunrise. I'd wear an extra shirt under my coat. My Da would swing his pick up on his shoulder. I had nothing to carry, so I stuffed my hands deep in my pockets. In the dark, we'd follow our familiar path to the road. My Da told me you don't have to see the road, just feel it with your feet. Stay on the road and you wouldn't get lost. My Da wouldn't talk, so I followed his example.

On a clear night, I'd watch the stars disappear into the sunrise as I followed the sound of my Da's footsteps. I was getting over my fear of banshees in the dark. I figured they wouldn't come after me as long as I was with my Da and his pick. Besides, what were banshees compared to the ghost of Cor Hegarty who now haunted my dreams.

We traveled north. More men joined us on the road. There were nods, but few words. I don't know how many miles we walked as the sky brightened. We came to the top of a hill and in the valley below there were hundreds of men. From so high up they looked like ants. We went to join them.

A man in a black flock coat and tall hat sat at a wooden table. He brought the table with him in a wagon in the morning and would take it home at night. He wore gloves with the fingers cut off so he could write down our names. You had to give your name to be paid. He'd write all the names down in his ledger. Men, like my Da, who brought their own picks or shovels, were paid more.

If the sun was above the horizon when he wrote down your name, you were docked half a day's pay for being late.

Men came from all over the countryside to work the road. We were one of the lucky ones who still had our coats and caps. Many men, especially those who lived closer to Skibbereen, had pawned their coats to buy food for their families. I was cold just to look at them. Some wore clothes that they never took off. They were so battered and tattered that they were no better than rags. Their stink made me want to hold my breath.

Once we signed in we'd find men from our own village. We worked by their side. My Da's job with his pick was to break rocks apart on the hillside. Some were as big as a boulder. I was given a basket and the chore to carry the broken rocks from the hillside to the end of the lane where boys, some younger than me, set the rocks in the road. Men didn't want women to work on the road with them, but some still did. If a wife lost her husband what else was she to do?

It was hard work, but no harder than what I was used to. Before my brother Paddy left, we cleared the stones from my uncle's fields and used them to build a stone wall to mark the field's boundaries. Most of the men who worked the road were used to hard labor. It wasn't the work that did them in, but the lack of food. The English supplied neither food nor water for the workers. Many men had no food to bring with them and toward the end of the day some would collapse where they stood.

My Da and I had dried meat from the pig that we carried in our pockets. I learned quickly never to chew jerky in front of the other boys. I couldn't bear the stares of those who had nothing. It would have been Christian to share, but I wouldn't. My Da taught me well, we had to keep what was ours to survive.

There was a creek not far from the road. The water was free and cold. I'd sneak away for a drink and sit by myself on the bank and chew my jerky.

I remember how excited I was at the end of the first day that I worked with my Da on the road. My wages would be the first money that I earned on my own. I hoped they'd give my earnings to me and not to my Da. I wanted to give the money to him myself, money that I earned to help feed our family.

I turned in my basket as did the other boys. Men who didn't have their own shovels returned the spades the British had given them. I stood in line by my Da to be signed out and collect my day's wages, but there were no pence for me or my Da. The pay would be at the end of the week, not at the end of the workday.

Men shouted and argued, but what were they to do? At least, I knew I had a bowl of soup to go home to, but what of those men who had nothing? How would they be able to come back tomorrow?

We left in the dark and came home in the dark. My legs ached with each step on the way home. My Ma had the soup ready. I was past being hungry. All I wanted to do was sleep, but my Da wouldn't let me leave the table until my bowl was empty.

I remember I saw his face when he carried me to bed and when he woke me the next morning.

Chapter 11

One day was much like the others. I was tired and hungry all the time. My muscles ached when my Da woke me in the morning. It wasn't until we started walking that my arms and legs would lose their stiffness. Some mornings, I was so tired that I walked with my eyes half closed and felt like I was dreaming in the silence of the predawn.

Each day there were fewer of the men who had no coats and no food. I tried not to think of what became of them. But there were always new men to take their places.

Toward the end of the first week, I just wanted to give up. I wanted to tell my Da that I wanted to stay home in the warmth of my bed. But when he shook me awake in the morning and looked into my eyes, I couldn't refuse him.

What kept me going through the day was the thought of the money that I was earning: Money that would buy food.

We stood in line at the end of the long week and waited for our wages. Angry shouts came from the front of the line. One man lifted the recorder's table and smashed it to the ground. The man in the black coat scrambled for his ledger. He grabbed the book and ran to his wagon. His hat flew off, but he left it. He jumped up into the wagon and whipped the horse down the road to Skibbereen

News spread like fire on a thatched roof, we would not be paid until the end of next week. Men who survived the week knew they might not survive the next. They couldn't go home without money to buy food for their children. They screamed and shook their shovels at the sky. I had never felt such anger coming from so many men.

One man shouted, "There's food in Skibbereen."

My Da put his hand on my shoulder and kept me by his side. He was as angry as I've ever seen him. Men walked around us and then stomped down the road to Skibbereen.

"What are we going to do?" I asked.

My Da seemed torn by indecision. "I fear no good will come from this." He swung his pick up on his shoulder. "But we have to do something." He squeezed my shoulder. "Stay close to me."

I nodded.

We became part of the angry mob that marched to Skibbereen.

From the top of the rise, I saw the flash of light reflected off the bayonets in the setting sun. An officer sat on a white horse that pranced back and forth in front of the soldiers. There must have been 100 soldiers that blocked the main road into Skibbereen. They were lined up in two rows that stretched from one side of the road to the other. As we got closer, the first row of red-clad soldiers kneeled. The soldiers all had muskets that they held at the ready. The officer moved to the side of the lane out of the way of fire.

We stopped. I could clearly see the soldiers' faces. I recognized some of the soldiers who were born and raised in Skibbereen. I suddenly realized what was going to happen. At the officer's command the soldiers would fire. I pictured the plumes of smoke rising from the muskets. I wondered if I'd feel the bullet. I realized a pick or shovel is no match for a musket. I wondered how many of us would die from just one volley from the 100 soldiers.

The officer drew his sword and raised it above his head. My Da pushed me behind him. I peeked out around his coat. In the silence, I heard a stream of water that pooled beneath the pant leg of the man who stood next to me. I felt an unbearable urge to turn and run.

"Stop!" The shout came from behind the rows of soldiers.

There was movement and then a man appeared by the officer's horse. It was Sheriff Galway, the Justice of the Peace. He grabbed the horse's bridle and said, "Let me talk to them."

We stood like statues afraid to breathe.

The officer slowly lowered his sword, but didn't put the sword back in its scabbard. Sheriff Galway walked to us. The officer steed pawed the earth.

CHAPTER 12

My Da carried his pick on one shoulder and a bag of corn on the other. Mr. Galway listened to our pleas and convinced the merchants to give us grain now to be paid for later when we received our wages. On our way home we passed a number of men who collapsed in the road. They could barely walk much less carry a bag of grain.

Mr. Wholey sat at the crossroads. His eyes were vacant as he stared at the road under his feet. One hand protectively clutched his bag of grain. He was from our hamlet. I was surprised when my Da stopped.

My Da set his pick and bag of grain on the ground and squatted next to him. He said, "Jerry, you need to get the food home to your family." He helped him to his feet. Mr. Wholey's legs quivered. His face was pale and his breathing rasped from his lungs. He reached for the grain, but couldn't lift it.

"Easy does it, Jerry," said my Da. He lifted Mr. Wholey's bag and put it on his own shoulder. "Danny, put our bag on my other shoulder." He bent and I did what he asked. "You take the pick." I lifted the pick and swung it up on my shoulder. "Now take his hand, Danny,"

I didn't want to.

My Da stood with his back bent by the weight. His arms curled up and around both bags of grain. I withered under his stare. I reached for Mr. Wholey's hand, but when I touched his hand, he pulled away.

"It's OK, Jerry," my Da said. "Let Danny help you. We'll get you home."

I took Mr. Wholey's hand. I could feel every bone beneath his skin. When he looked at me, I don't know what he saw.

My Da turned and started down the lane. We followed. Mr. Wholey shuffled more than walked. His breathing sounded like two tree limbs that rubbed together. The pick dug into my shoulder and made my arm go numb.

My Da would walk a ways and then stop and wait for us to catch up. I saw a look of deep concern in my Da's eyes. I thought he must have known Mr. Wholey his whole life. Maybe they were friends when they were kids like Cor and me.

Mr. Wholey let go of my hand when he saw his cottage in the gloaming of the evening. He caught up to my Da. Together they walked to the cottage's door. My Da bent and set our bag of corn outside the door and then carried Mr. Wholey's bag inside. I set the pick by the door and followed them into the cottage.

The single room was warm, but the stench was unbearable. Mrs. Wholey sat at the table. Her eyes went from her husband to the bag of corn. Tears rolled down her cheeks. It was an effort for her to stand. She went and put another cut of peat on the fire.

The Wholeys' children huddled in bed. I thought they might be scared of strangers. Their eyes followed me as I walked closer to them. I realized the stench in the cottage came from their bed. The smell belonged outside in a privy. The oldest struggled to sit up on the edge of the bed. She pushed the covers back on the other children. From long, dirty, straw hair, I knew she was a girl but she had the figure of a boy. Her eyes were like little black coals sunken into her ashen face. With a look of surprise, her hand covered her mouth. I thought she must have seen the corn. Her fingers reached into her mouth and came out with a tooth. She held the tooth in front of her. She looked like she didn't know what it was.

"Danny, we need to go," my Da said from the doorway.

The girl tossed the tooth to the floor. She struggled to stand. Her clothes were soiled. I slowly backed away. She ignored me as she walked to the fire.

My Da waited outside. He had our pick on one shoulder and the bag of corn on the other. I gulped fresh air as if it were water. My Da turned to go.

I said, "I'll take the pick,"

He stopped and looked down at me.

"I can carry it, Da."

He lifted our pick from his shoulder and put it in my hands.

CHAPTER 13

Toward the end of another day of work, the wind changed. During the day the wind had come from the southwest, as it normally did in winter. Now, it swirled down from the northeast. It was cold - so cold it hurt my chest when I breathed. Thick clouds blocked out the sun.

The snow started while we stood in line to have our names signed out. If I wasn't so cold it would have been beautiful. Some years we'd go a whole winter without ever seeing a snowflake. Now within minutes, the ground was covered with a radiant, white blanket.

We signed out and my Da said, "You must keep up, Danny. We have to get home quickly,"

"Why, Da?"

"A storm's coming the likes of which you have never seen."

He took off at a fast pace. I had to jog to keep up with him. We got to the top of the hill and the wind blew stronger. It howled in my ears. Snow pellets stung my face. It looked like a white swirling wall was coming for us across the valley.

My Da swung the pick down from his shoulder and said, "You stay behind me and hold onto the pick." He shouted above the wind. "Don't let go of the pick."

I grabbed the head of the pick. He turned and held the handle at his side. I walked behind him and held onto the pick that connected us. His body blocked the force of the wind. Snow swirled around us. The snow was so thick that I could barely see his back.

Within a short time the icy snow was so deep I couldn't even feel the road beneath my feet. We'd walked the road many times. I knew my Da must be walking from memory because there was no road to be seen.

The snow deepened and I struggled in his footsteps. I entered a world I'd never imagined, a world of complete whiteness. My hands and feet were past the point of being cold - they were numb. I don't know how I held onto the pick.

Snow rose above my feet and felt frigid on my ankles. My ears stung and ice coated my eyelashes. I tried to bury my face into the protection of my coat. I had to lift my feet above the snow to step in my Da's snow prints. We struggled on.

I lost track of time. I don't know if we walked for minutes or hours. My Da stopped and I bumped into him. He turned. White ice coated his beard and eyebrows. He looked lost and afraid. He peered into the surrounding whiteness, but there was nothing to be seen. Snow was up almost to my knees.

"Give me the pick," he said.

I released the pick. He lifted it and swung the blade down into the snow. He cleared a spot and then knelt and pushed his hand through the snow to the ground.

He stood and shouted, "We're still on the road. We'll keep the wind to our back to find our way home." He extended the pick to me. I grabbed ahold. He turned and set off with me tethered behind him.

My teeth chattered. The wind wailed. The sky blackened with the coming of the night.

The wind died, but snow still fell in the growing darkness around us. Everything was deathly still. My Da stopped and I stopped with him. I was beyond cold. Now, I was so tired that I just wanted to lie down and sleep.

My Da peered into the dark.

"Danny." He pointed. "Do you see anything?"

I looked where his finger pointed. I squinted.

"Is it a fire?" I asked.

"I'm not imagining. You see it too. It's a torch, Danny."

Chapter 14

My Da swung the pick up on his shoulder and grabbed my arm with his other hand. He pulled me through the knee deep snow. I helped as much as I could, but my feet felt like lead. Snow swirled and we'd lost sight of the fire. My Da never slowed. He kept trudging forward.

We walked and the feeling of intense cold returned. It felt like the cold was not outside, but now inside my body. There was a sharp pain in my lungs with every breath that I took. My teeth chattered so hard that I thought I would break them.

I stumbled, but my Da wouldn't let me fall. Ice pellets stung my face. My hands were so cold that I couldn't move my fingers. We followed the light from the torch until the fire went out.

I awoke in front of the fire. My head rested on my Ma's lap. Her hand covered my ear. I lay under the covers between two warm bodies.

"Is he going to live?" Mary's voice said from behind me.

"Hush," my Ma said.

I drifted back to sleep.

Hunger woke me. They said I slept for two days. I sat at the table and slurped bowl after bowl of soup that was mostly water. The tips of my fingers were purple. Michael sat across from me and stared at me as if I was a stranger.

Now that it seemed that I wasn't going to die, my sisters lost interest in me. They played with Brigid in their sleeping area of the cottage.

My Da sat and stared into the fire. I finished my soup. He got up and walked behind me and tousled my hair. He sat on the bench next to me.

"How did we get home?" I asked. "I don't remember."

"Your Ma lit another torch. I followed the light with you on one shoulder and my pick on the other."

I shook my head. "I don't remember."

"Sometimes it's best you don't."

My Ma took my empty bowl.

"Is God punishing us?" I asked.

My Ma exclaimed, "Why would you say that?"

"He destroyed our potatoes and now he sent the storm so we can't work on the road."

"It's not God's will, son," My Da said.

"Then who's to blame?"

We all looked at my Da and waited for his answer. He got up from the table. He walked and sat in his chair and stared into the fire.

CHAPTER 15

The sun returned. The wind shifted so that it came from the southwest. In our cottage, there were puddles on the floor from the snow that melted on the roof and seeped through the straw. It was still cold, but not the bitter cold of the storm.

We couldn't work on the snow-covered road, but they paid my Da half his wages to just come and break stones. That's what he did. There was no work for me, so I stayed home.

Michael and I ventured out onto the snow-covered fields. Sun reflected off the snow and hurt my eyes, but the countryside was beautiful. Everything was radiant white and pristine. The girls joined us. Brigid wanted to go home and see her folks so we all went with her.

Brigid's Ma fed us and that was a welcome surprise. With Caitlin gone to America, the boys gone to Cork and Brigid spending most of her time with my sisters there was only the two parents left in the cottage. They had some corn left where ours was all but gone. Brigid's Ma made a corn stirabout that was like porridge. After weeks of eating soup it tasted delicious. I felt like there was something in my stomach besides water.

Brigid wandered away from the table to her bed. She brought a box back to the table and sat between Joanna and Mary. In the box there was a brush and a comb.

"Were they Caitlin's?" Mary asked.

Brigid nodded and fingered the brush.

"I wonder where they are now," Joanna said. "They've been gone for four months."

Mary added, "Caitlin said she would write."

"She will," Brigid's Ma said.

"I bet they have plenty of food," Joanna said. "There're probably staying in a grand house with Paddy's uncle." She laughed. "Maybe Caitlin's with child."

Mary gave my sister a look and then shot a quick glance to me and Michael.

"What?" Joanna said. "There're married. She should be with child by now."

"The Good Lord willing," Brigid's Ma said.

They fell silent. Then Mary said in a soft voice, "I wish I was with them."

"Me too," Joanna added.

"Paddy said he would get a job and send money so that we could all go to America," I said.

"If he sends money," Mary said, "It'll be for you. You're the oldest boy. You'll go next."

I didn't know what to say. I didn't know if my sister was jealous or mad.

"I've some cornbread," Brigid's Ma said to Mary. "It's hidden away. I've been saving it. Let's have the bread today. We'll worry about tomorrow when it gets here." She went to get the bread.

I looked at Michael. He looked at me and his face lit up like it was Christmas.

CHAPTER 16

The snow melted and I returned to work on the road, but the storm had taken its toll. Hundreds of men didn't return. It seemed every day bodies of men who were lost in the blizzard and never made their way home were found in the fields. There were scores of older and weaker men who simply did not have the strength to return to work. Every day our number dwindled.

Somehow my body kept growing. Our workdays grew as the sun stayed in the sky longer. My legs were stronger from walking and my arms from lifting and carrying. March came, and with it came the hint of spring. Between my Da and me we barely made enough money to put food on the table. The price of corn had doubled from what it was last year. My Da never thanked me when I gave him my wages, but I never expected him to.

Our lives went on and we existed day to day until the day came when it all changed again.

I grew to love the early morning mix of silence and sound as the earth came awake. Small birds sang from bushes and then fluttered over our heads. Some mornings, fog lay close to the ground and I felt like I was walking through clouds.

We were almost to the road at the start of a new workweek when I asked, "Da, this road we're building, where's it go?"

He laughed. "Only the British know. The men all say we're building a road that goes nowhere."

"But it must go somewhere?"

He laughed again and shook his head. I don't know if he laughed at me or at the British.

We came over the rise and looked down to the valley. Men stood in groups where the front of the line should be, but there was no sight of the registrar. His cart and horse and table where not to be seen.

We joined the men. The sun rose over our heads while the laborers made small talk and waited. It was midday when Sheriff Galway rode up on his horse. He didn't need to call us. We all walked toward him.

He stayed on his horse and shouted, "They'll be no more money for the road. You best go home now."

A shocked silence followed his words. I struggled to understand what he said. Without work on the road we'd have no wages. We wouldn't have money to buy food. We'd surely starve.

One man shouted, "We want to work!" Other laborers took up the call. "We want to work! We want to work!" More joined in. They banged their shovels and chanted, "We want to work." Like a mob they surged toward Sheriff Galway.

The uproar spooked Sheriff Galway's horse. The Sheriff pulled his pistol and fired it up into the air. The men quieted.

The Sheriff settled his horse and then shouted, "The British will give no more money for the road."

My Da shouted, "We'll have no money to buy food."

"There is nothing I can do," Sheriff Galway said. "But let me tell you this," he waved his pistol in the air, "The British brought another detachment of Dragoons to Skibbereen last night. The town's an armed camp. If you march on Skibbereen they will surely kill you."

Sheriff Galway's words chased the fight out of the workers. The mob vanished and all that was left was a group of scared hungry men. The Sheriff holstered his pistol. His face changed as he stared out at the defeated laborers. Some of the men he had grown up with. He looked sad. I felt that he wanted to say more, but he just turned and rode away.

My Da stormed away from us and walked over to the middle of the road. He lifted his pick and smashed it down on the gravel. Again and again, he gouged the stones. He tried to destroy what we built. Men stared, but no one would go near him. Sweat beaded his brow, but still he slashed the road. I stood and watched. I didn't know what to do.

My Da dropped his pick and collapsed. He sat on the ground and buried his face in his hands. I went to him and sat beside him. I couldn't see his face. His shoulders shook. Men walked around us on their way home.

CHAPTER 17

"Da, we need to get home. It's getting dark."

My Da sat on the road with his pick by his side and looked at me. He seemed as if he came from a place faraway.

"It's not fair to you, Danny," he said. "Your childhood shouldn't be like this. Mine was a happy childhood. We'd plant our potatoes on St. Patrick's Day. We'd weed the fields as they grew, but we also had plenty of time to play. It was a good life. In many ways it was an easy life. The potatoes would feed us all through the year. In spring we'd plant the seed potatoes and our lives would go on."

He lifted a pebble from the road and threw it out to the field. "We brought it on ourselves. We never should have depended on just the potatoes. But what choice did we have? Our farms are so small. The only crop that could feed our families was the potatoes."

"It's not our fault, Da. The British are to blame. There's plenty of food in Ireland. No one would starve if they'd let us keep the food that's grown in our own land." I lifted the pick that lay between us. "People in Skibbereen aren't starving. They have plenty of food."

"Did you not hear Sheriff Galway," said my Da. "The soldiers are waiting. You go against the British and they'll kill you. Your Great-Grandfather tried to rid us of the British and it got him hung. We're farmers. The British have their army and their cannons. We have our picks and shovels. We'll never beat them."

"Does it matter if they hang us or starve us, we'll still be dead."

My Da took the pick from my hand. "You need to survive. Your brother's in America. Paddy will send money and you'll join him. You'll have a life there."

He stood and swung his pick up on his shoulder. He grabbed my collar and pulled me up. I walked beside him on the road that we built, the road that went nowhere.

CHAPTER 18

Without the wages from the road, we had no food. Days passed. I got to the point where I stopped feeling hungry. I had no energy to do anything. I spent most of my day in my bed and wished for dreams to take me away.

I awoke one afternoon. I saw my Ma by the hearth stirring a pot. She spooned out a potato. I knew I had to be dreaming, but I didn't want to wake up. My ma put a steaming bowl of potatoes on the table. She saw I was awake and called my name. I realized I wasn't dreaming.

My Da came home from another day of looking for work where none was to be found. I'll never forget the look on his face as he saw us sitting at the table with the potatoes. My Ma stood up from the table and went to him. His look of surprise suddenly turned to anger as he understood what she had done. He grabbed my Ma and shook her.

"What have you done?" he screamed. "We can't eat the seed potatoes."

My Ma broke free and pushed him away.

She pointed to the table. "Look at your children. They're starving."

My Da shook his fist in her face. "If we eat the seed potatoes we'll have nothing to plant."

My Ma's anger matched his. She slapped his hand down. "They won't live to see the harvest."

With her words, it seemed like my Da crumbled before my eyes. He wearily shook his head and went and sank down on his chair by the fire.

I knew the terrible price that we were paying. By eating the seed potatoes now, the only potatoes that were spared from the blight, we would live, but without the seeds we would have nothing to plant.

My Ma filled my Da's bowl with potatoes. She carried the bowl to him and set it on his lap.

Chapter 19

It was through the kindness of strangers that we survived. The seed potatoes were gone and the earth was still barren. It was heartbreaking to be starving and visit the strawberry patches. No matter how hard I'd stare at the blossoms, strawberries would not suddenly grow in front of my eyes. I didn't know if we would survive to taste their sweetness. If only spring would come.

I awoke to find my Da in his chair by the hearth. I wondered why he had not gone on his daily search for work. There was not a morsel of food left in our cottage. My Ma sat at the table with her eyes closed. She rocked back and forth with her hands clasped together. I wondered if she was praying. I got out of bed and walked to my Da. He wouldn't look at me.

"Wake you sisters and brother," he said in a cold voice. "Tell them to get ready. We're going."

I was afraid to ask where.

We walked to Skibbereen. We didn't have the energy to talk so we were silent. With no food in our stomachs, God must have thought we suffered enough for one day. He pushed the rain clouds away and brought the sun out that dried the road beneath our feet. My sisters walked together, one supporting the other. Michael's legs gave out halfway to town. My Da carried him. I don't know how he found the strength.

We joined hundreds of Irish farmers on the road to Skibbereen. Some of them seemed like dead men and women walking. They were all skin and bones clothed in filthy, rotten rags. The smell was unbearable. Old men sat by the side of the road and stared at us. They could go no farther.

We crossed the river and joined the line. There must have been thousands of people that waited outside a large stone building at least four stories high. I don't know how many hours we stood in line and slowly inched forward to the Steam Mill. Some people were so weak that they crawled on their hands and knees.

One man shouted words that no one understood. He was crazy from hunger. His eyes were wild. He yanked the hair on his head and shouted louder. Men pushed him out of the line. When he tried to get back in line, a man punched him. The crazy man fell to the ground and curled into a ball.

We finally gained access to the large hall. The room was lined with tables and at the tables sat the Irish with their bowls of soup.

A worker stood on a platform and stirred soup in a pot that was taller than Michael. Women handed bowls of soup to us as we passed. The room was filled with the sound of slurping soup and spoons clicking on bowls.

The benches were full. We waited our turn. When an empty seat on the bench appeared someone was there to quickly take it. We were lucky, a family left and we took their places. There wasn't enough room so Mary and Joanna sat at another table.

I tried to savor the soup, but I couldn't. I quickly slurped it down. I desperately wanted more, but one bowl was the limit.

Michael ate slowly. He looked at the vegetables on his spoon and stared at them in wonder.

My Da ate with his head down. He wouldn't let his eyes meet anyone else. He was a proud man. To be dependent on the charity of others was not his way.

I glanced at the surrounding tables and wondered if we looked like the others, if we too were one foot away from the grave. Many hands shook as they struggled to lift their spoons to their mouths. One man spilled a spoonful of soup on his beard. He lifted his beard and tried to suck the soup into his mouth.

There must have been hundreds of us farmers in the room. I gazed around and tried to figure out what was missing. I looked at Michael beside me and then glanced around again and then I knew. There were no young toddlers or babies for their mothers to nurse. If they weren't here, where were they? I didn't want to know.

There was a commotion at the end of our table. A man finished his soup, stood, and collapsed. Workers came and tried to rouse him, but he wouldn't wake up. They carried his still body from the room. Another man took his place at the table.

Others were waiting. We could not linger. As soon as Michael finished, we stood and walked to the door. Another surprise awaited us. As we left, we were all given a piece of bread. I couldn't believe it. I wanted it to save it, but I couldn't. The bread was gone before I walked outside.

CHAPTER 20

We left the soup kitchen. The soup revived us. Michael found his legs and even smiled. My Ma took Michael's hand and led him down the street. She wasn't going home. We all knew where she was going. My sisters followed. I waited for my Da to see what he would do. He took his cap off and ran his hand through his hair. He gave a soft belch. I could see the cross atop the belfry from where we stood. My Ma was halfway down the street when he decided to follow. I followed him.

My Ma walked up the stone steps. She turned and waited on the landing. The stature of St. Patrick was behind and above her on top of the porch of the entrance to the church. St. Patrick had his hand out in blessing or in welcome. The girls joined her. My Da's foot hesitated on the bottom step. He would go no farther.

He gave me a shove. "Go with your Ma, Danny."

St. Patrick's Church towered over Skibbereen. I joined my Ma. At the top of the steps, I could see the whole town and the farmland beyond. My Ma looked down at my Da and gave him a look. I don't know if it was disappointment or sorrow. She covered her head with her shawl as did my sisters and we entered the church.

St. Patrick's Church was the grandest place that I had ever seen. My Ma told me it took four years to build and that my brother Paddy was one of the first infants to be baptized in the church. I entered the large wooden doors. No matter the weather, it was always cool inside.

The church was crowded with many more women than men. My Ma led us as close as she could to a pew near the altar. It was as if she tried to get as close to God as she could. We kneeled and my family joined the praying of the rosary that had already started and seemed to continue forever.

I said the words, but my mind was elsewhere. I never tired of looking at the inside of the church to try and figure out how it was built. I studied the high ceiling and wondered why the stones did not fall down upon us. How could a man create the images captured in the stained glass windows? It was all beyond me.

The rhythm of prayers surrounded me. My knees went from pain to numbness. We stayed until Michael whispered to my Ma that he had to pee.

I took Michael to do his business. We came back and joined my Ma and sisters at the bottom of the church steps. My Da stood among a group of farmers in front of a shop across the lane. He was deep in conversation with the men. Some of the men were from our hamlet. We walked to him and waited, but he ignored us. Clouds came and with them came a soft rain.

My Ma kept looking anxiously from my Da to Michael. I knew she worried about my brother more than the rest of us. He seemed so weak and fragile. He didn't seem to be growing.

"Tell your Da, we're going home," my Ma said. She took off her shawl and wrapped it around Michael's head and shoulders and led him and my sisters away.

I knew better than to disturb my Da. I leaned against the store front to try and get out of the rain. It was getting dark before my Da was ready to go. I walked by his side on the way home. My mind was filled with questions.

"Da, who were those people who gave us the soup?"

"The good people who live in town. They still have their jobs and money. When the potatoes rotted, they tried to feed the starving that came begging. But there was too many to feed. The Quakers came and gave them the caldron and taught them how to make soup that could feed thousands. And that's what they did. They say the Quakers have shamed the British into opening soup kitchens throughout Ireland. We won't grow fat off the soup, but it'll keep us alive."

"I don't understand. The last time we came here they were ready to kill us."

"Not them Danny, it was the British army that had the guns. Don't you understand anything? The town folk are Irish. They're not the damn British."

I felt chastised, but he was right, I didn't understand.

CHAPTER 21

Spring came. I awoke early, as was my habit. Michael had curled his legs over mine. Even in his sleep, he seemed to always be cold. I gently snuck away from him while he slept on. My Da was already gone. My Ma had our empty cooking pot ready for me on the table. I grabbed the pot and set off on my mission.

There were too many poor Irish farmers and it took too long to feed them all at the Steam Mill. So the good people of Skibbereen put pots in carts and filled them with soup. They drove the carts out to the countryside. My job was to take our pot and walk to the crossroads and wait for the cart to come along. I'd leave as soon as I awoke so that I could be the first in line. Sometimes there were so many people waiting that they ran out of soup and those at the end of the line went home hungry. I couldn't take that chance with my family. I had to be first.

I didn't mind getting there early. In the cottage there was always someone with me. At the crossroads, before the others arrived, I could be by myself. I'd sit and enjoy the silence. There was always something new to see; a bird's nest in the bush, a line of ants on the ground, bees dancing among the flowers. I'd watch the sun play peekaboo as the clouds glided across the sky.

The same man always drove the cart. When he stopped, his wife would get down and hand out the soup. I don't know if she took pity on me because I was always first in line. She'd scoop the spoon to the bottom of the caldron and come up with a spoonful of vegetables that she ladled into my pot. She was so different from my Ma and sisters. She smiled. Her apron was always clean and there was never a smudge of dirt on her hands and face. She smelled like flowers. I thought she was beautiful and kind.

People gossiped that the man and his wife were not our religion. I knew that there were people in town who would give you soup if you came to their church, but the man and his wife weren't like that. They never talked religion. They gave us food when we were starving. That's what I remember.

The first day they came to the crossroads, the wife asked me my name and I told her. Her name was Mary, like my sister. Every day she would greet me by name and ask about my family. Her husband's name was John. He sat in the cart and settled the horse while Mary handed out the soup. He wasn't a smiler. When he looked on us, he always seemed sad.

I always said both their names and thanked them for the soup. Many a day the soup was the only thing we had to eat.

It was a job to get the soup home. It took twice as long to walk home as it did to go get the soup. I couldn't walk too fast for fear of sloshing the soup over the side of the pot. The handle dug into my palm. I'd have to stop a dozen times and set the pot down and change hands.

No matter how hungry we were, we'd save the soup for evening when my Da got home. There were times when he'd bring some corn or rice home with him. My ma would mix the grain into the soup and reheat it over the peat fire. On those nights, I'd lie in bed with my stomach full and think that we might survive.

CHAPTER 22

It was too late. He saw me first. I almost dropped the soup. I couldn't run and hide. Coghlan stood next to a cart by our cottage. I tried to avoid his stare as I slowly walked forward. My Ma stood in the doorway with her arms folded across her chest.

"Your Da's not here, so you'll help me," Coghlan said.

He walked to the back of the cart. My Ma came and took the soup from me. Coghlan could easily lift the bags of seeds by himself, but he waited for me. I hated to go near him. He took one end of the bag and stared at me. I came forward and took the other end. He stunk of whiskey and smoke. We carried the bag and set it beside our cottage. He grabbed hold of my upper arm

"Where'd you get the muscles?"

I tried to pull away, but he squeezed harder. I squirmed. He laughed. His breath stank worse than a privy. He pushed me away and I tripped and fell. He walked and stood by the cart. I felt my anger coming. I got up and walked quickly to the back of the cart. I grabbed the end of a bag. I didn't wait for him. I yanked the bag from the cart. It was too heavy for me. It fell to the ground. I couldn't carry it by myself, but I could drag it along the ground. And that's what I did.

Coghlan pulled his pipe from his pocket. He leaned back against the cart and lit the pipe. He stared at me as I emptied the cart. I don't know what it was, but the way he looked at me as I worked was not the way a man should look at a boy.

My Da brought home a small bag of rice and my Ma mixed it with the soup.

"We'll have to plant the oats in the evenings," my Da said. "I still have to find odd jobs to do during the day. We can't live on just a bowl of soup." He lifted his empty bowl and tilted it to his mouth. He swallowed the last drops of soup. "If we have a good harvest we'll be able to pay the rent. That's why Lord Townsend gave us the seeds. He wants his rent. If we can pay the rent we can keep our farm."

I said without thinking, "What about the potatoes?"

My Da angrily shoved the empty bowl aside and gave my Ma a look. She got up from the table and took his bowl and then walked away. She wouldn't meet his stare.

"The seed potatoes are gone, Danny. We don't have money to buy any more. Even if we did, their price is too dear. But we're not alone. There's not a seed potato left in Skibbereen."

My Ma leaned over the bucket and cleaned the soup bowl.

He stared at my Ma. His voice lost its anger. "The others made the same choice we did. It was either eat the seed potatoes or die. We chose to live."

My Ma glanced up at my Da and both their faces softened.

"We can't eat the oats," I said, "because the oats pays the rent. If we don't have potatoes to plant what will we eat in the fall?"

My Da ran his fingers through his beard. I could see the worry in his eyes.

"We have the soup," my Ma said. "Let's be thankful for what we have."

CHAPTER 23

Summertime came and we settled into our routines. My Da scrounged for work as best he could, but it didn't seem to help much. Prices for food were so high and with every man trying to find work, wages were so low. The pay for a full day's labor wouldn't even buy a small bag of corn. My Ma and sisters took Michael with them to the fields to search for anything they could add to our bowl of soup. Come rain or sunshine, I made my morning pilgrimage to the crossroads. The pot of soup I carried home was the only constant in our lives. The soup kept us alive through the summer.

I set the pot of soup on the table and covered it with a towel. My job was done. It was now time to go explore to see what else I could bring home for my family to eat.

Our hamlet was not the village that Paddy and Caitlin had left behind. Now, there were so many empty cottages. Some still stood, but many were tumbled.

One day, I watched from afar as Coghlan and his men set to work with their crowbars on the Donnels' home. When the roof collapsed, they burned the thatch. By the end of the day, all that was left of the cottage were mounds of rubble on the ground. I couldn't see his face, but I knew Coghlan had to be giving his wicked grin. I was surprised that he didn't dance a jig on top of the ruins. He was getting his wish to turn our farms into pasture. I don't know what happened to the Donnels and other families like them, but I knew they'd never come back.

There were times I got to an empty home before Coghlan, but I'd never go inside the cottage. I was too afraid of what I'd find. Cor still haunted my dreams. How many other cottages were filled with dead families? I didn't want to know.

I didn't think what I did was stealing. There were berry patches near some of the abandoned cottages. The families were gone so they weren't there to hoard the hidden treasure. They were on his land, but I knew Lord Townsend wasn't going to come and pick them. So I figured it was finders-keepers.

When I found the first patch, I couldn't stop eating the blueberries. They were so sweet. The juice stained my fingers. I felt guilty. I wanted them for myself. I didn't take the berries home to share with my family. I knew where they were and that I could go again the next day and have my fill. I stopped by a stream on the way home and washed the evidence of my crime off my hands and face.

That night I couldn't sleep. Michael lay in slumber beside me. His breath was soft against my cheek. I was overcome with guilt. He needed the berries more than I did and yet I deprived him. What sort of brother was I? What would my Da say if he knew? I tossed and turned the whole night.

In the morning after I returned with the soup, I snuck off with our bucket. I went back to the patch and no matter how much I wanted one, I didn't eat one berry. Bees buzzed around me as I filled the bucket. Part of me wanted the bees to sting me, but they just went about their business.

The bucket of blueberries was on the table when my family returned home. I can still see the look of delight on Michael's face. That night I fell asleep before Michael did and I slept through the whole night.

CHAPTER 24

We'd wait for my Da to get home before we had our soup. Soon as we were finished with our meal, my Da and I would head out to our fields. Sometimes Michael would tag along. Our days were long and nights were short in summer. The oats were planted, but they still needed to be weeded. The grain grew fast.

We had no seed potatoes to plant so we tried to plant oats in our potato fields, but the oats wouldn't take hold. Potatoes could thrive on our rocky sections of ground, but not oats.

As we weeded, I'd catch my Da staring at the empty field next to ours. I knew what he was thinking. It we could plant oats on that field we might have enough food to survive.

At one time the field was ours. My Da's brother didn't want to be a farmer. Uncle Richard left and gave the right to farm the land to my Da. Uncle Richard went to America and settled in Philadelphia, where he became a blacksmith. When the potatoes rotted, Paddy and Caitlin went to stay with him.

My Da wanted to plant oats on my Uncle's land, but when Gale Day came he didn't have enough money to pay the rent on both our land and my Uncle's. We kept our home and land, but lost my Uncle's. Coghlan got his wish. He turned my Uncle's land to pasture.

My Da went back to weeding. We needed our oat crop to pay the rent on the next Gale Day. If we couldn't pay the rent we'd lose our home.

CHAPTER 25

Fall came and our lives changed once again.

We sat at the table. We just finished our soup. Brigid ran into our cottage with a smile wide on her face and burst out, "Uncle Seamus..." She had to catch her breath from the run from her cottage. "Ma says for you to come. He has a letter from Caitlin."

My Ma made the sign of the cross on herself. She quickly got up. She went and grabbed her shawl and was out the door before we knew it.

Brigid's cottage was smaller than ours, but their table was just as big. With Caitlin and her brothers gone there were empty seats. Uncle Seamus sat at the table with a bottle of whiskey in front of him. Next to the bottle was his fiddle. He hadn't changed at all from the last time I saw him. He got up when he saw my Da. They walked to each other and embraced. I thought Uncle Seamus was the same age as my Da, but my Da looked so much older.

Uncle Seamus stepped back and studied my Da.

"It is good to see you, Joseph," he said. "These are hard times. You'll share my whiskey. I brought the bottle from Cork." He saw me and said, "Does Danny still have the voice of an angel?"

"We've had no time for singing," my Da replied.

"There's always time for music, Joseph. That's what keeps us alive."

My Ma couldn't wait for pleasantries. "The letter," she said. "Is Paddy and Caitlin well?"

"We'll find out together, Maggie." Brigid's Ma caressed the letter as she stood by the fire. "I didn't want to open it alone."

My Ma nodded that she understood.

Sarah walked to my Ma and took her arm. "I don't think I can stand while I read it. Let's sit at the table."

They moved to the table and sat on the wooden bench side by side. Sarah's hands shook as she said, "To think this letter came from Caitlin all the way across the ocean to be in my hand."

She crossed herself and so did my mother and so did I.

We all stared as Sarah slowly opened the envelope. Inside the envelope there were white pages and a strange looking paper, the likes of which I had never seen. She held the colored paper up to Uncle Seamus.

He smiled and said, "It's a U.S. Banknote. It's money."

Sarah quickly scanned the first page. She smiled as tears ran down her cheeks.

"They're in Philadelphia. They're safe."

The two mothers hugged each other as they both cried.

CHAPTER 26

Brigid's Da rapped his knuckles on the wooden table.

"Get on with the letter," he said. "We're all waiting."

Sarah wiped tears from her cheeks. She took a deep breath and began.

My Dearest Family,

I hope this letter finds you well. I can't believe the stories we hear about home. I hope that none of the stories are true, but I fear they are.

Paddy and I are well. A storm at sea nearly took us, but the Good Lord brought us safely here. Uncle Richard and Aunt Elizabeth are so kind. They have a grand house. Their children are grown and they have their own homes, so Paddy and I have a room to ourselves. The winter is bitter cold here, but the house is warm.

Paddy is helping Uncle Richard in the shop. There is plenty of work for a blacksmith. Paddy's always been a hard worker. Father O'Malley at St. Joseph's Church found me a job. A parishioner, Mrs. McCloskey, is old and crippled. I clean her house and do her laundry and tend to her needs. She is sweet, but sometimes she can't remember who I am.

Life is so different here. It is so loud and noisy and crowded. I so yearn to just walk in our quiet fields.

Here everyone has food the like of which you'd only find on
Lord Townsend's table. How I wish I could share it with you.

Sarah set the page down and picked up the next page of the letter. Mary and Joanna sat across from me at the table. They had such a wistful look on their faces.

Uncle Richard will take no money for our room and board.
Paddy and I have saved every penny that we have made to
send home. Paddy promised me that he would send for Brigid
when we were settled and now we are. My heart broke when I
left my dear little sister. I need her with me to heal it.

We all turned to Brigid. She was only seven. I didn't know if she understood what the letter meant to her and her future.

Paddy wants Danny to come with Brigid. Paddy says Danny
can clean the shop in the evenings, during the day he will go to
school. In America there are those who can read and write and
those who can't. Uncle Richard said you can give the banknote
to the captain of any ship going to America. It will pay the
passage for both Brigid and Danny.

I was shocked. I was beyond speechless. Everyone stared at me. Mary glared at me. I didn't know what I did to her. She pushed away from the table and fled the cottage. Joanna took after her. My Ma sat there with her lips tight and watched them go.

You don't know how much I miss you. After my prayers, I cry
myself to sleep every night thinking of my Ma and Da, James
and Dennis, my dearest Brigid and Ireland.
Paddy will keep working so we can bring you all to
America. I will work as long as I can, but I am with child.

Sarah caught her breath. Her hand went to her chest. She and my Ma exchanged a look and their eyes watered.

I need to get this letter off so that you know we are safe in America and so you can send Brigid and Danny to us.

Please know that I love and miss you all deeply. I will write more later.

CHAPTER 27

My Da sat quiet. I couldn't read his face. I didn't know if he was happy that I was to go to America or not. My Ma still had tears in her eyes from the news of Paddy and Caitlin's baby. I think she also had fresh tears for me.

"Thomas, do you have a glass?" Uncle Seamus asked. "Or should we just pass the bottle?"

Sarah got up from the table. She returned with three mugs. Uncle Seamus poured a few ounces into each mug. He pushed one to my Da, one to Brigid's Da, and kept one for himself.

Michael said to Brigid, "Let's see if the fireflies are out."

They got up from the table and ran across the room and then outside into the late evening twilight.

My Ma and Brigid's Ma left the men with their whiskey. They went and sat by the fire and talked in low voices.

I didn't know what to do. I felt too old to play with Brigid and Michael. I sat at the table and waited for my Da to send me away, but he didn't. I sat still and listened as the men talked.

Uncle Seamus downed his whiskey. He poured a few more ounces into the cup and said, "They shut the soup kitchens down in Cork."

"What?" my Da said. His voice was a mixture of surprise and anger.

"The British said they'd only keep the kitchens open until the harvest and now the harvest is here."

"What are we to eat?" Thomas said.

"You'll have your potatoes."

"We have no potatoes," my Da said. "How do you think we survived the winter?"

"None at all?" Uncle Seamus shook his head like he couldn't believe what he heard.

"If we didn't eat our seed potatoes we would have died," My Da said.

Uncle Seamus looked to Thomas.

"It's the same for all of us," Thomas said. "No one has potatoes."

"Good Lord," Uncle Seamus said with a look of dismay.

"What is it you're not telling us?" My Da asked.

Uncle Seamus stroked his beard and stared at my Da. "There'll be no more soup kitchens. It's the work of Trevelyan, the devil himself. He governs the British Treasury. The British may rule us but they will not feed us. Trevelyan said, 'Irish property will pay for Irish poverty.'"

His voice harsh, my Da almost shouted, "We own no property."

"They'll tax the ones who do: the landlords and merchants. The increased taxes will go to the workhouses. To get your soup you'll have to give up your land and go into the workhouse."

My Da slammed his mug on the table. "I'll not give up my land."

CHAPTER 28

Uncle Seamus took up his fiddle. He closed his eyes and started to play. I remembered the last time he was here. It was my brother's wedding and wake. It was the last time we were all together as a family. Paddy and Caitlin married and left the next day for America. It was the last happy time that I could remember. Uncle Seamus played his jigs. Neighbors came and danced outside the cottage. Caitlin was beautiful and I'd never seen my brother so happy. Now Caitlin and Paddy were gone and so were most of our neighbors.

The music called Brigid and Michael to the cottage. They sat together on the floor near the hearth by their mothers. Uncle Seamus' music has always moved me. It's like the music gets inside me. Sometimes it makes me want to dance and sometimes to cry. I could listen to his music forever.

I felt her stare. I turned and saw my Ma watching me. She smiled and I smiled too. I thought of the times we'd sing a song together at night when she came to tuck me in. How I missed those nights.

Uncle Seamus started a new song and then stopped. I knew what he wanted, but it had been so long since I'd sung. My Da wasn't a singer, but he knew the words to the songs handed down from father to son in our family for generations. He taught me the words so that I could sing for him. Uncle

Seamus started the melody again. The last time I'd sung the
song was the night before Paddy left. The music touched and
filled me. The song was the story of my Great-Grandfather.
It was a song of love and parting. My Great-Grandfather was
hung by the British in our rebellion of 1798.

I stood and words came from within me. I sang,

"The Minstrel Boy to the war is gone
In the ranks of death you find him;
His father's sword he hath girded on,
And his wild harp slung behind him;"
"Land of Song!" said the warrior bard,
"Tho' all the world betrays thee,
One Sword, at least, thy rights shall guard,
One faithful harp shall praise thee!"

My voice was no longer the voice of a child. I don't know what
it was. I wouldn't look at my Da because the song always made
him cry.

CHAPTER 29

I couldn't sleep. My mind was filled with too many thoughts. I tossed and turned from my side to my back to my side. Michael was out like a candle, but even in his sleep, when I'd settle for a moment, he'd try to snuggle next to me to seek my body's warmth.

When we were little, I was jealous of the way my mother and sisters treated Michael like he was special. He was the baby. I picked on him and we fought all the time, but I couldn't win. Paddy always took his side.

But that all changed when the potatoes rotted and Paddy left. I became the big brother and I looked at Michael through different eyes. It was my job to protect my little brother and keep him safe.

I worried about Michael more than anyone else. No matter how hard the last year was, I still grew. My pant legs where halfway up my shins. But Michael's clothes haven't changed. I don't think he has grown at all.

I gently pushed the hair from his forehead. His breath was soft on my arm. When I go, he'll have no one to cuddle next to. He'll be cold throughout the night.

I tried to picture my Uncle Richard's grand house and a table with plenty of food: to picture a life where you didn't go to bed hungry.

In Caitlin's letter, Paddy said I'd go to school in America. I'd never been to school. I don't know what school would be like. But I would like to learn how to read and write a letter and maybe learn how they build a church.

Michael stirred and cried in his sleep. I put my arm around him and held him close. I wondered what would happen to my little brother when I'm in America. If Uncle Seamus is right and they don't bring soup to the crossroads, how will he survive?

CHAPTER 30

When Paddy left we had a wedding. When I left we had a wake.

Michael was sullen. He knew I was going away and leaving him behind just as Paddy had. When we finished our morning soup, he sat at the table and stared at me. He wouldn't come near me.

There wasn't anything for me to pack. It was cold enough that I could just wear my extra shirt under my coat. My Ma sat on my bed. She seemed so sad. I didn't know what to say. She had a letter in her hands, but it wasn't Caitlin's letter.

She held the letter out to me and said, "Give this to Paddy." She must have seen how confused I was.

"Sarah took my words and put them on paper."

I nodded that I understood. She put the letter inside my coat pocket.

We were all supposed to go to the city, but Mary refused to come with us. Mary was like my Da. When she made up her mind she wouldn't change it. It hurt me so the way she looked at me. It wasn't my fault that I was going to America and she wasn't.

Joanna walked to me and held out her scarf. She wrapped it gently around my neck and then stuck the ends inside my coat.

She hugged me and said she would pray for me every night. I said I would do the same.

Joanna told my Ma that she would stay with Mary so that her sister wouldn't be alone. I expected my Ma to argue, but I don't think my Ma had the energy for a fight.

My Da stood at the doorway and stared at us. He was never a patient man. I expected Michael to stay with my sisters, but my Da wanted him to come with us. He wanted Michael to see the ships that hopefully one day would take him away from Ireland.

My Da pointed to Brigid's house and said, "They're outside waiting for us."

My Ma took her coat from the wall peg and put it on. She gave one of her looks to Mary and a different one to Joanna. She lifted her hood and walked out the door.

I took one long look around our cottage and tried to put it all in my mind.

"Danny." My Da's harsh voice broke my trance.

We left the cottage. We were halfway to Brigid's house when Mary caught up to us. Her fierce hug caught me by surprise. She looked at me as if she was trying to memorize my face. She didn't say a word. She quickly turned and ran back home.

CHAPTER 31

There was a two-wheeled cart and donkey next to Brigid's cottage. Coghlan sat on his horse and watched as we approached. He had a grin on his face. His teeth were black in his mouth. He looked to my Da and then at me. I refused to look away from his stare. His gaze went up the hill. Mary was almost to our cottage. Joanna came out and met her. I was glad that Mary wasn't alone. Coghlan returned his gaze to me. He made my skin crawl. He turned his horse and then rode off.

"Brigid's too small to walk all the way," Thomas said. "But she's too big for me to carry."

"I know Coghlan wouldn't let you use the cart for free," my Da said.

"He didn't," said Thomas in a tone that implied that he didn't want to say anymore.

Sarah lifted Brigid and set her on top of a layer of hay that covered the bottom of the wooden cart. She said, "There's room for two. Michael, why don't you climb up?"

Michael looked to our Da. When he didn't say anything, Michael ran and scampered into the cart. Brigid's eyes lit up as if it were all a game. The donkey lurched forward and tossed one child against one other. They both laughed.

We set off down the lane. My Da and Thomas each walked on one side of the donkey. I walked behind the cart next to my Ma and Sarah.

Sarah said to my Ma, "Brigid thinks she's just going to visit Caitlin." She turned to me as she added, "I didn't have the heart to tell her anything else and neither did Thomas."

I nodded that I understood. I thought maybe it was better that way.

"It breaks my heart," Sarah said. "But there's no life for her here never knowing where we'll get our next meal. At least with Caitlin, I know she'll have food in her stomach. She'll be safe with her big sister. She can help with the baby..."

The coming loss seemed to hit Sarah all at once. My Ma took her arm. They slowed and put some distance between them and the cart so that Brigid would not see her mother's tears.

We spent one hour after another walking the lane. When Michael or Brigid grew restless they'd stop the cart so the children could walk. My Ma or Sarah would take their place and sit on the back of the cart with their feet almost touching the ground.

We walked through deserted hamlets and I wondered if this is what war looked like. The cottages were tumbled. There wasn't one stone left on top of another. The stones were covered with a heavy layer of soot from the burned thatch roofs. The people were gone. I wondered where they went. Cows, too many to count, grazed in the fields next to the rubble.

We walked by fields of golden grain. Laborers were out in the fields harvesting the crop. It seemed like the fields went on forever. I didn't understand why we were hungry in the land of plenty.

We got closer to the port city and that's where we found the Irish who were driven from their land and had their cottages tumbled. They weren't in the city, but on the outskirts. They lived in ditches along the side of the road. Some families had dug holes into the side of the ditch. It looked like they lived in caves. Even in the daylight, smoke came from their peat fires. Other families used branches to prop thatch above their heads to keep the rain away. The smell was overwhelming. I was used to the stink of pig manure, not that of humans.

The people looked like skeletons. What little clothes they had just hung from their bodies. They were so dirty their skin looked black. I couldn't understand why some of the children had swollen bellies when their arms and legs looked like twigs. There were children who looked like their hair had fallen out of their heads and started to grow on their faces.

Their eyes followed us as we walked by. Out of nowhere the fear came upon me. I was suddenly so scared that my hands were shaking. If we lost our farm we'd have no choice but to join the homeless. I looked to my Da. He stared at me. I went and stood next to him and we walked on together. It was all I could do not to hold his hand. I knew he was the only reason why we kept our farm. He was all that stood between my family and being homeless.

We were almost to the city. It dawned on me that that's why the homeless were in the ditches. They wouldn't let them stay in the city so they stayed as close as they could to the soup kitchens. From their hovels they could walk - or if they had to, crawl - to get their bowl of soup and piece of bread.

I hoped Uncle Seamus was wrong. If the British closed the soup kitchens, what would the homeless do? If the British closed the soup kitchens, surely these people would die.

CHAPTER 32

We didn't find Uncle Seamus, he found us. His clothes made him stand out from the laborers and farmers who wore clothes no better than dirty rags. The homeless wandered the crowded city streets as they searched for work or handouts. One look at Uncle Seamus and you knew he wasn't a farmer. It was one of the few times I saw him without his fiddle. He walked up and touched my Da's shoulder. I never really noticed before, but his hands were clean - even his fingernails. His hands were his livelihood and his trade was his fiddle. No matter how hard the times, there was always a bar or a street corner where men would give a few pence to hear Uncle Seamus play his music to drown out their sorrows. His gift was that he could play his fiddle, but I think an even greater gift was that he knew how to listen.

"Have you found a ship?" asked my Da.

"There's only one ship in port that's going to New York. The rest are all going to Liverpool. The ship's a clipper like the Liberty."

Uncle Seamus stared at me. "Are Danny and Brigid well? The captain fears the Black Fever. He won't let them on his ship if they're sickly."

"The children are fine," my Ma said. She crossed herself as she said the words.

"Then follow me. There's a family you need to meet."

Michael and Brigid's eyes filled with wonder as they saw the ships. I had been here before when Paddy and Caitlin sailed away, but the sight still stirred me. The closer I got to the ships the more anxious I became as the reality sank in that I was leaving my home forever.

Uncle Seamus left us on the dock. He disappeared into the wooden sailing ship. There was a constant swirl of motion around us. Seamen rolled barrels up a wooden plank onto the deck. Flags fluttered from the tall masts that looked as barren as trees in winter.

Uncle Seamus returned with a young couple. They couldn't have been much older than Paddy and Caitlin.

"This is Francis and Julia Meagher," said Uncle Seamus.

Sarah lifted her daughter from the cart and set her by her side. Michael climbed down and stood next to Brigid.

Julia walked up to the young girl and said, "You must be Brigid." She squatted so that they were face to face. "I have four sisters and four brothers. One of my sisters is about your age. Her name is Ellen. She's has blue eyes like you." She smiled and adjusted Brigid's bonnet. "You're such a pretty girl." She straightened and turned to Sarah and my Ma. "We come from big families," She nodded to her husband. "But we're all alone going to America. We'd be happy to have the children with us. I hear it's such a long voyage. We wouldn't be so lonely." She took a step and squatted by my brother. "And this must be Danny."

"No, that's Michael," said my Ma. "Danny, come here."

Michael looked up at me. I saw the future in his eyes.

CHAPTER 33

I ignored everyone else and walked up to my little brother. I lifted his chin and stared into his eyes. I knew what I saw was true.

I said, "Michael will go and I will stay."

"Danny, don't talk nonsense," said my Da in a hard voice. He came forward and towered over me.

My anger came and I couldn't stop it. I stared at my Da and said in a voice harder than his, "If I stay here I will survive, if Michael stays, he won't." I grabbed Michael's shoulder and pushed him in front of my Da. "Look at him and tell me I'm wrong."

My Da's face slowly changed. He put his hand gently on Michael's head.

"There's only death for him here," I said. "If he goes to America, he'll live."

My Da gave a small nod. The anger left me. I turned my little brother toward me. He seemed beyond bewildered. I took off Joanna's scarf. I gently wrapped it around his neck and tucked the ends inside his coat.

"You're the big brother now," I said in a soft voice. "Brigid is family, it's your job to go with her and protect our little sister." I reached inside my coat and took out my Ma's letter. "You need to give this letter to our brother. Can you do that?"

Michael looked at me and then at the letter and nodded. I slid the letter inside his coat pocket. I took a breath and stared at him. There were other words I wanted to say, but none would come to my lips.

My little brother threw his arms around my neck and clung to me. I didn't want to cry, but I did.

CHAPTER 34

I gently released my brother's arms from my neck and stood up straight. Everyone's eyes were upon me.

I faced the young couple and said, "Michael gets cold at night. He needs someone to snuggle next to."

There were tears in Julia's eyes. She said, "We will take care of him as if he was our own."

"You have my word on that," her husband added.

"When you get to New York," my Da said, "You can send a letter to Philadelphia. I'll give you the address. Paddy will come and get his brother and Brigid."

"I can't write," Francis said, "but I'll find someone who can."

Uncle Seamus said to my Da, "We need to see the captain so you can take care of the children's fares. They'll be papers to sign so Thomas and Francis, you need to come too."

"The rest can come with me," Julia said. She tried to smile amid the sadness. "I'll show you our new home for our crossing over the ocean."

"I'll stay here," I said. "Someone must watch Coghlan's cart and mule."

I expected my Ma or Da to argue, but neither did. They must have known I had no more goodbyes left in me. I watched my little brother. He held my Ma's hand as he walked up the gangway. He stopped at the rail and turned back to me. He looked so small on the large ship. I lifted my hand and he did the same. I wondered if I would ever see him again. My Ma put her arm around his shoulder and then they disappeared into the ship.

CHAPTER 35

I sat on one of the stumps that they used to tie the ships to the wharf. I felt empty inside. I wondered what my life would be like if I had chosen to go to America. I could be in the new world with Paddy. I wouldn't be like Francis. I would go to school and learn so that I could write my own letters. I wouldn't always be hungry.

I kicked my heels against the stump and chased the thoughts away. I had made up my mind and I wouldn't change it. I saw in my little brother's eyes that he would die if he stayed here. I had no choice. I had to try and save him.

I heard hoofs clatter on cobblestones. I saw horses come around the corner from behind the shops. The British officers sat high above me on their steeds with their swords at their sides as they rode by in front of me. The foot soldiers followed them with muskets on their shoulders and not a smile to be seen on their faces. Their hats made them seem even taller and the color of their uniforms always reminded me of blood. Their shoulders were broad and I knew their stomachs were full.

Horses pranced and soldiers marched along the wharf to the ship moored next to ours. Wheels rumbled under carts full of grain. A crowd of woebegone Irish followed the carts. Children searched the ground for corn that fell like golden nuggets from a few of the bags that split from the rough ride on the wagons.

Soldiers made a human barricade between the carts and the hungry. Seaman came off the ship and loaded bags of grain on their shoulders and carried them up the planks. I thought about how long my family could live on just one bag of grain. I looked from one ship to the other. I couldn't understand. In the hold of one ship our Irish grain was on its way to England. In the hold of the other ship, Irish who had no food to eat were on their way to America.

There was a commotion down by the corner. A man wearing a dark coat and vest stood on top of a wooden box in front of a shop. A crowd of unruly Irish surrounded him. He shouted and pointed at the seamen who carried grain from the carts. More Irish were drawn by his voice. I couldn't make out his words, but I didn't have to. His face was fierce red under his top hat as he shook his fist at the soldiers. I climbed on top of a timberhead built into the wharf so I could have a better look.

Everyone was watching the speaker. I noticed two boys, not much older than me, sneak up to the last cart in line. They each grabbed a bag of grain from the back of the cart. They weren't strong enough to carry the bags. They struggled as they tried to drag the bags along the ground. One boy tripped backwards and the bag of grain fell on him. The second boy stopped and waited for him. A soldier noticed. He raised his musket and fired at the boy who was still standing. How he missed the boy, I don't know. The boy dropped his bag and ran. Another soldier fired and then another. The boy, faster than I ever could, ran out of sight behind a building.

The other boy tried to squirm out from under the grain bag that pinned his legs to the ground. Two soldiers were quickly upon him. They yanked him to his feet. The boy's face was a white mask of terror.

With the shots, the crowd scattered. They ran everywhere except toward the soldiers. The man who stood on top of the wooden box was the only one who stayed. He screamed words I couldn't understand. He raised his hand to the sky and then pointed his fingers at the soldiers as if he tried to bring down God's wrath.

The stink of gunpowder filled the air around me. I should have run like the others, but I didn't. I jumped down and crouched behind the timberhead. I wanted to know what would happen to the boy.

The soldiers dragged the boy to their captain. One soldier knocked the boy's cap off and pulled him up by his hair so the captain, still mounted on his horse, could see the boy's face.

The soldier asked, "Do you think he's too young to hang?"

"That's for the magistrate to decide," the captain replied.

The boy shook so hard that I expected his bones to rattle. I could feel his fear, but there was nothing I could do.

CHAPTER 36

My Ma and Sarah held each other's arms as they walked down the plank from the ship. Brigid's mom's eyes and nose were red from sobbing. They stood together on the wharf and cried on each other's shoulders. My Da, Uncle Seamus, and Thomas stood off to the side to let the women share their grief. But they weren't alone. Other families lined the dock sharing the heartbreak of the partings. I couldn't see Michael or Brigid. They were out of sight in the hold. I said a prayer for their safe crossing. That's all that I could do.

We gathered around the cart.

"We've come this far," Thomas said to my Da, "Sarah wants to go to my brother's to see the boys before we come home. She needs to know that James and Dennis are well. Can you take the cart back to Coghlan? I can't afford to keep it for another day. We only needed it for Brigid." He stopped as he said his daughter's name and looked to the ship. He rubbed his fingers against his chin.

"I'll make sure Coghlan gets the cart and donkey," my Da said.

Thomas nodded his thanks. He shook hands with Uncle Seamus. He took his wife's arm and led her away. Sarah kept looking back to the ship as new tears streamed down her cheeks.

My Da said to me, "Since you stayed, I'm going to go to England. There are too many men and no work here. Uncle Seamus says they need workers for the harvest in England. I'll only be gone a couple weeks." His eyes glanced to my Ma and then back to me. "We have no potatoes. If they close the soup kitchens we won't survive the winter unless I have money to buy food."

He was looking at me, but I felt like he was also speaking to my Ma.

"I'll spend the night here. There's a ship off to England in the morning. You need to get the cart and donkey back to Coghlan and take care of the farm while I'm gone. Can you do that?"

I didn't know what to say, so I just nodded.

He walked up to me and put his hands on my shoulders. "If you had gone and Michael stayed, I wouldn't go. I couldn't leave the family alone. But you're here."

I was only 11 years old, but suddenly I felt so much older.

Uncle Seamus knew a shortcut to get us through the city. He took hold of the donkey's bridle. He had a way with animals just as he did with the fiddle. I walked next to him. My parents walked far behind the cart. They didn't want me to hear them argue. I knew my Ma didn't want my Da to go. There were stories in our village of other husbands and fathers who went to England for the harvest and never came back. I knew my Da would come back to us. The only reason he wouldn't was if he was dead.

We walked past the homeless who waited for their daily bowl of soup.

"Will they really close the soup kitchens?" I asked.

"They will in the fall," replied Uncle Seamus.

The line of homeless stretched as far as I could see.

"We still have no potatoes, why would they close the soup kitchens now?"

"Danny, you have to understand the ways of the world. Now the British can get grain from America as cheap as from Ireland. They have their corn, now they want their meat. You can't ship cows across the ocean, but you can ship cows across the Irish Sea. They want our land to grow their cows. To get our land we must be gone. It doesn't matter to them if we starve to death or flee to America. All that matters is that they get our land. I fear one day they'll be more cows in Ireland than Irish."

"It's not right."

"It hasn't been right for 700 years. The English rule the land. They'll do what they want."

CHAPTER 37

We continued down the road past the city shops. I realized there were only two types of people in the city: those who had money and those who didn't; those who wore fine clothes and those who wore rags. The shops were full of merchants selling and people buying. The smell of roasting meat mixed with the aroma of baking bread. My stomach growled so loud Uncle Seamus looked at me and smiled. I couldn't understand why some people were starving while other people were growing fat.

Uncle Seamus stopped the donkey and said, "Wait here."

He walked to the market. He had to walk through the destitute who gathered by the doorway with their hands out to beg for food or coins.

My Ma and Da came up to the cart. It was strange the way my Da looked at me. I felt as if he was seeing me for the first time. I wanted to go with him to sail on a ship and see a new country. I worked with him to help build the roads, so I figured I was old enough to harvest grain in England. But he asked me to stay. When I thought about it, I knew he was right. When we worked the road we were always home at night. If I went with my Da we would both be gone for weeks. Times had changed in Ireland. It wasn't a time to leave women on their own especially with our neighbors, Thomas and Sarah, being away. There were always men the likes of Coghlan.

Uncle Seamus came out of the shop. He carried two wrapped packages. He gave the parcels to my Ma and said, "It's not much. It's only a couple loaves of bread and a small slab of bacon. It's all that I could afford."

My Ma pushed the packages back. "I can't take these."

Uncle Seamus held his hands up. "Maggie, you keep them. It's a long walk back home. Danny needs food. He's a growing ...I was going to say boy, but I don't know if he's a boy anymore. But don't eat the food here." He cocked his head toward the beggars by the shop's entrance. "It's not right to eat in front of them."

Uncle Seamus turned to my Da. "Joseph, you come with me. It's time to fiddle for my dinner. They'll be enough to share and whiskey to go with it."

My Ma started to cry again. My Da walked to her. He took the packages from her and put them in the back of the cart. He took my Ma in his arms and hugged her.

"I do what I must," he said.

"I know you do." She stroked his beard. "The Good Lord bless and keep you safe."

My Da let my Ma go and walked to Uncle Seamus. My Ma lifted the packages up from the cart. She thought, like I did, the food wasn't safe in the back of the cart with so many starving around us. She would keep the food with her until we were out of the city.

My Da nodded to me. I went and took the donkey's halter and waited until my Ma joined me. Together, we led the cart away. I glanced back to my Da and wondered, like I did with Michael, if I would ever see my Da again.

CHAPTER 38

We stopped when the city was behind us. My Ma opened Uncle Seamus' gift. She broke off a hunk of bread and gave it to me. She took none for herself. She went and sat on the back of the cart and stared forlornly at the distant masts of the sailing ships. I left her to her sadness and led the donkey down the lane.

I walked on as the sun sank to the horizon. The countryside was beautiful as falling light played gently across swaying amber fields. The world had gone silent except for a slight breeze that tickled my ears and the soft rumble of the cart's wheels on the stones.

Clouds covered the sky and darkness descended upon us. Without the moon and stars, I knew there was no way we'd find our way home. I led the donkey off the road to a field near a tumbled cottage. I tethered the donkey. I took some hay from the bottom of the cart and set it near his feet.

The cold came as the sun set. I sat on the ground with my back up against the cart's wheel.

"Danny, it's too cold on the ground," my Ma said. "There's enough room for you here."

I stood up and she moved back into the cart. I climbed up and laid on my back next to her.

"Your Da can say what he wants, but you're still my little boy." She put her arm across my chest and snuggled next to me. The side of the wooden cart kept the wind from us and my Ma's body heat kept me warm. With the sun set, the darkness quickly surrounded us. I couldn't see my hand in front of my face. Even with my Ma next to me, the fear of the banshees came. The dark came alive with their whisperings, farther off came their shrieks.

I wondered if the family who had lived in the tumbled cottage was buried under the rubble. Did they starve to death like so many others? Would their ghosts come out of the ruins and walk around the field by our cart to search for potatoes that were no longer there?

I couldn't sleep until the rising sun chased the shadows from the field.

My Ma shook me awake. I felt like I hadn't slept at all. We set off for home. My Ma's spirits were better. She walked beside me and sang as our world bathed in the sun's glory. Sometimes I took for granted Ireland's beauty. I joined her in song. It wasn't long before she stopped and listened to my voice. I sang. With my Ma beside me and the beauty around us, at least for a while, I felt happy.

St. Patrick's Church was on our way home. I knew my Ma would have us stop and I was right. She wanted me to go inside with her and join the rosary with the women who seemed to fill the pews no matter what time of the day. I pleaded that I needed to stay with the cart and watch the donkey and our food. But the truth was I didn't want to join the women. I'd never been much for prayer. I needed to use my hands, not hold them still in prayer.

I knew my Ma was disappointed. She reluctantly left and walked up the steps. I had no doubt that she would pray for my soul as she knelt by the altar.

Time passed. The donkey grew restless and so did I. The donkey wanted to get home for a proper feed. To take him home meant I had to take him back to Coghlan.

CHAPTER 39

There were two towering buildings in my youth. One was St. Patrick's Church and the other was Lord Townsend's Manor House. Each building created its own sense of awe. I had been to St. Patrick's Church more times than I could count. I had only been to the Manor House once. My Da always took Paddy, his oldest son, with him when he went to pay the rent. When Paddy left, my Da took me.

From the outside, the Manor House was just as majestic as St. Patrick's Church. I don't know anyone who had ever gone inside the Manor House, but I guessed the inside must be just as grand.

Lord Townsend came from England and visited his estate only once a year. People said he came to Ireland just to take our money back to England. I'd never seen him, but my Da said he saw him once from afar when he was a boy. Lord Townsend rode in his carriage and was dressed in his proper finery.

Mr. Nelson ran the estate for Lord Townsend and it was to him that we paid our rent. We didn't pay the rent at the Manor House, but at the carriage house, which was built off to the side. My Da said Mr. Nelson was a hard man, but fair.

I led the donkey down the winding road to the Manor House. In the field, men stacked stones one on top of another. I watched them as I approached. We built fences to clear the

stones from our land and mark our boundaries. The workers
weren't building a fence. They were building a wall of stones
that was higher than their heads. The wall extended around the
grounds of the Manor House. I wondered why Lord Townsend
felt he needed to build a wall.

A man sat on a horse and watched the workers. He noticed
me and rode toward me. I knew the man had to be Coghlan.
As he rode closer, he recognized me. I'll never forget the look
of surprise on his face.

"I thought you were off to America," he said.

"I let Michael go in my place."

His eyes lingered on me.

"What are doing with the cart?"

"Thomas asked me to bring it back to you. He and his wife
went on to see their sons. He said he'd be back in a few days."

"Come with me." He turned his horse and I had no choice
but to follow.

I had never been this close to the Manor House. Inside the
stone walls, there were gardens the like of which I had never
seen. It was turning fall, yet the flowers still bloomed. Beautiful
flowers were arranged in neat rows. Each different type of flow-
er had its own section in the garden. Girls, who wore long
dresses and white bonnets, knelt in the rows and picked weeds
between the flowers. I thought it was so odd. If you wanted to
see flowers all you had to do was walk in the countryside. You
didn't need to plant them in front of your house.

The Manor House loomed over me. Countless windows reflected sunlight that gleamed like stars. I wondered how many
rooms were inside and how many people could live there.

We went past the house to the stable. A boy, not much
older than me, came out from the stable to take the donkey.
I thought there must be something the matter with his legs

because he limped as he walked. He kept his eyes fixed on the ground as if he was afraid to look at Coghlan.

"Timothy," Coghlan said. "Put the cart away and make sure the donkey gets fed. Snap to it now. There're plenty of other boys who would be happy to take your place and have food in their stomachs." He looked at me and asked, "Isn't that right, Danny?"

The boy seemed suddenly afraid.

Coghlan laughed. "Ah, but Timothy's a good boy. He does what I ask him and never complains. He also knows how to keep his mouth shut. Isn't that right, Timothy?"

Timothy said in a small voice, "Yes, Mr. Coghlan." He walked toward me, but he wouldn't meet my eye. He took the donkey's halter and led the cart to the stable.

Coghlan edged his horse closer. He leaned over me. I smelled the stink of his breath.

He said in a voice that only I could hear, "There's always a job for a boy who will do whatever I ask."

I felt the evil in him. I didn't know what he wanted and I didn't want to find out. I wanted to run as fast as I could to get away from him, but I didn't. I met his stare and shook my head.

Coghlan laughed, but there was no humor in his laugh. "Mark my words, boy. There'll come a time when you're hungry enough, you'll come begging for work and then you'll do what I ask." He pointed to the boy who limped to the stable. "You'd be amazed at what a boy will do when he gets hungry enough."

He wheeled his horse. The sudden movement caught me by surprise. The horse's flank knocked me to the ground. Coghlan laughed again. His was a boisterous laugh. He rode his horse toward the stable and the boy inside.

I clenched my fists. I wanted to chase him and pull him down from his horse. I wanted to stomp my foot on his face. But I knew I wasn't big enough and if I tried I'd be the one who was stomped. I snatched my cap off and slapped it against my leg. It felt like my lungs were on fire. Again and again, I drew a breath in and pushed it out.

I turned and walked away.

CHAPTER 40

I waited at the crossroads. I wondered if this would be the day when the soup wagon didn't come. As the sun rose, others joined me, but I was first in line as always.

I was glad to be out of the cottage. With each additional day that my Da was away, my Ma got crankier. My Da had been gone for two weeks, but it felt like two months. We expected him to be gone, what we didn't expect was for Thomas and Sarah to be gone as long as him. They said they'd just be a few days with their sons. My Ma visited their cottage every morning. She returned silent and glum. Sometimes, I felt she was more worried about Sarah than she was about my Da.

At the crossroads, there were rumors of a new sickness in the city. Beside Black Fever there was the looseness. You couldn't control your bowels. You would lose anything you ate or drank. You'd void yourself until your body shriveled and died. Of all the ways to die, I thought that must be the worst.

I feared for Brigid's parents. When people go away, you never know if they'll come back.

I saw the soup cart and suddenly the day brightened.

I set the bucket of soup, covered with a towel, on the table. Our field of oats was growing and soon would be ready to harvest. With luck, we'd have enough money to pay the rent and maybe a little for food. Until the harvest there wasn't much for me to do. My Ma and sisters were out searching for roots to add to the soup. Sunlight poured through our doorway.

The thought came upon me out of nowhere. If I left right away, I could go to the ocean and surprise my Ma by gathering seaweed. My Ma would dry the seaweed and we'd all eat it like a treat. Maybe that would brighten her spirits. I grabbed some twine. If I could find enough, I could tie the seaweed together and carry it on my back. I would be home before dark. I was already out the door before I finished the thought.

My Da always said you had to be half-goat to make the walk to the ocean. Following the lane from our cottage was easy through the fields, but when the lane ended, there was a steep, winding path down the cliffs to the ocean. I knew I had to be especially careful. There was no one with me. If I turned an ankle, how would I get home?

I stood on top of the cliffs. I could stand there forever and gaze at the ocean. The sparkling white tops of the waves hypnotized me. The ocean had no end - it just disappeared into the sky. The wind blew. I could taste the salt of the sea on my tongue. I carefully descended the jagged path to the rocky sand below.

I wasn't alone. I shouldn't have been surprised. People combed the shore. Children ran barefoot into the cold sea and grabbed seaweed from the surf. They ran back with the treasured seaweed to their mothers. Most of the people seemed to be families. At the base of the cliffs there were makeshift shelters that were made of thatch propped against the sheer walls. The thatch would help to keep the rain and wind away. Smoke rose from cooking fires. I wondered how long the people were here and if they could survive the coming winter.

The coastline stretched as far as I could see. The ocean went forever. The families claimed this spot and I didn't want to take their food from them. I figured I'd try my luck farther down the shore.

CHAPTER 41

I walked along the shore. I had never been this far down the coast. The sun was high overhead. Part of the cliffs jutted out into the ocean and I couldn't see what was beyond them. My curiosity got the better of me. I climbed over the rocks at the base of the cliff. On the other side of the rocks was an inlet. In the inlet there was a boat.

I climbed down from the rocks to the sandy shore. A fisherman stood in the middle of the small boat and cast a net. He brought it up empty. The waves pushed the boat closer to shore as he cast again. I stood and watched. The waves pushed his boat to shore in front of me.

The fisherman saw me and shouted, "From the looks of you, you're not a fisherman, so you're here either for the clams or the seaweed." He jumped from the boat and easily pulled it up on shore.

He was a small man, not much taller than me. He wore a thick coat and floppy hat. Above his scraggly beard, his face was lined and deeply tanned from the sun. His eyes were like black raisins.

"You don't have anything to dig clams with so it must be seaweed you've after." He pointed to a rocky outcropping down the shore. "That's where you'll find the seaweed."

"Did you catch any fish?" I asked.

He laughed and gave me a funny look. He beckoned me with his finger. I walked toward him. He pointed to a dozen or so small fish in the bottom of the boat. Some of the fish were still gulping and thrashing.

He pointed his finger out to the ocean. "The big fish are out there. Some of them are bigger than my boat."

I felt the side of the boat.

"It's just cowhide. You've never seen a curragh before."

"Not up close."

I traced my hand along the wooden slats on the inside.

He said with a hint of pride, "My family's been fishermen for generations."

The wind picked up and with it came the waves that crashed on the shore and rocked the curragh against the sand.

"As good as she is she's no match for the ocean, not when the ocean gets mad. I have to stay close to shore."

"Are there a lot of fish out there?"

He laughed and I felt like a fool for asking.

"There're more fish out there than all the potatoes that have ever grown in Ireland."

His face tightened and I noticed the lines around his eyes as he stared at the vast sea.

"But I can't get at them. My boat's too small. You need a proper boat to go way out and fish the ocean." He spit to the water but the wind carried his spit back by to his feet. "I don't know an Irishman who has a boat big enough to fish the ocean." He laughed. "The fish in the ocean have nothing to fear from the like of us."

He studied me. "Where're you from?"

"Carrigillihy."

"I've never heard of it."

"It's just a small clachan south of Unionhall."

"I've been to Unionhall."

I looked to the sun in the sky. "I better go. I need to get some seaweed and get home before dark."

"Do you want some fish? I have enough to share."

"I wouldn't know what to do with them."

He laughed and then pointed to the rocky outcropping. "The seaweed is yours for the taking."

He pushed his boat back into the water and got in it. He used an oar to push away from shore.

He shouted as he got farther away. "Down past the seaweed you'll see the round tower of the old Monastery. You can't miss the path that goes up to it. Follow the path past the Monastery and it will take you to the road to Unionhall. It's a lot quicker than going back the way you came."

I waved my thanks. He turned from me and dug his oar into the water and fought against the waves.

CHAPTER 42

Waves pushed seaweed to shore where the rocks trapped it. Picking the seaweed was easy; the hard part was not to slip off the rocks. I quickly gathered as much as I could. I used the twine I brought from home to wrap it in a bundle. I tossed the seaweed up on my shoulder and then stood on the shore. I looked up and down the coast to try and commit this spot to memory. I knew the ocean waves would always drive more seaweed to the rocks.

I continued down the coast. You couldn't miss the tower. It jutted above the cliffs like a fat arrow pointed at the sky. There was a well-traveled path that led from the ocean to the top of the cliff. It was steep, but not that hard of a climb.

Next to the tower were the remains of a church. The ceiling was long gone, but the stone walls still stood. I walked through the doorway and stood in the center of the church. I tried to picture what it was like to pray here centuries ago. Did they have pews to kneel on or did everyone stand? The walls were empty. I wondered if way back then they had statues of the saints. I turned in a circle and that's when I saw him.

He was a tall, gaunt man whose long, dark cassock blended into the wall behind him. The top of his head was bald. There were white turfs of hair on the side of his head. He had no beard. He held a staff in one hand. He had the most piercing blue eyes that seemed to stare right into my soul. I didn't know whether to run to him or away from him.

I blurted out, "I didn't mean to disturb you. I'll go."

He held his hand up and walked toward me. I couldn't tell if his robe that went down to his feet was dark brown or black. He wore a white rope as a belt.

"It is I that did not mean to disturb you, my child."

He made the sign of the cross with his right hand. I bowed my head.

"My name is Brother Brendan and I'm on a pilgrimage. What brings you here?"

"I came for the seaweed down at the ocean. A fisherman told me the path by this Monastery is a quicker way home."

"And where is home?"

"Carrigillihy. It's south of Unionhall."

"Unionhall is on my way. I'm going to St. Fachtna's in Rosscarbery, where I hope to spend the night. Come, we can walk a ways together."

He led me through the doorway. Next to the church there were piles of stones that reminded me of cottages that were tumbled.

"What happened to the Monastery?" I asked.

He stopped and looked out to the ocean. "The Vikings came. From up here the monks could see them coming. That's why they built the tower. The early Vikings came for plunder. The brothers would hide from them in the tower until the Vikings grew tired of waiting and went away. The Vikings who came later didn't come for our treasures, they came for our land. The Vikings were fierce fighters, but they were no match for our Irish women. The Vikings who stayed here fell under the Irish maidens' spells. The Vikings who stayed became part of us."

He looked at me. "That's where we get our blue eyes. They were a gift from the Vikings. There is Viking blood mixed with your Irish."

"I never knew the story."

"I fear there's much you don't know, son."

He pointed his staff at the scattered stones. "The Vikings plundered. It was the British who destroyed." He lowered his staff. "Come, we must not linger if you are to get home before nightfall."

CHAPTER 43

It was cool in the forest. Sunbeams danced among the leaves. It was quiet. Occasionally, I'd hear a bird cry. Brother Brendan was like my Da. He was a fast, determined walker. His staff moved in rhythm with his feet. I wondered how far he had traveled.

"Tell me about your family," Brother Brendan said.

"My Da's in England for the harvest. My older brother, Paddy, is in America. We just sent my younger brother, Michael, to join him. My sisters, Mary and Joanna, are home with my Ma."

He gave me a quizzical look and asked, "Why did Michael go instead of you? You are the next oldest."

I sighed. I didn't really want to talk about it. "Michael's not strong like me. I didn't think he would survive if he stayed here. So I asked for him to take my place."

Brother Brendan put his hand on my shoulder and turned me toward him. He stared at my face.

"How old are you?"

"I'm 11."

"You are old beyond your years."

He continued walking. "Now tell me about your family."

It was my turn to give him a quizzical look.

"Your ancestors. Surely, you must have stories."

I shrugged. "I have no stories of kings and castles. We're farmers. I don't know how long my family lived on our land, but I know we've been here for hundreds of years. The English came and took what was ours. I don't know when it happened. Now we pay rent so we can stay and farm the land that's rightfully ours. My Great-Grandfather fought in the rebellion of 1798 to take our land back. He was hung by the British."

"Yours is the story of Ireland."

He fell silent and walked on. I studied him as he walked. He was different. I'd never talked with a man like him. He seemed to search the forest off to the side of the pathway. Suddenly, he darted into the woods. I followed him.

He stopped at the base of a large tree. His eyes smiled in delight. There was a spread of mushrooms along the ground. He picked one and held it up to the light. He broke off a piece, rubbed it between his fingers, and smelled it.

"They'll do," he said.

His hand disappeared into his robe and came out with a cloth bag. I wondered what else he had in his pockets. He bent and picked mushrooms and slid them into the bag.

"Are you going to help or just stand there?"

I knelt beside him and soon the bag was full. He gave the bag to me to carry. He stood and stretched his back and then walked to a bush where butterflies danced. He stood and extended his finger. A butterfly landed on his hand. I held my breath. The butterfly's wings slowly opened and closed. He lifted it to the light. The butterfly flew away. I went to him and we walked together back to the path.

"Do you go to school?" he asked.

I was too embarrassed to answer so I just shook my head.

"The Vikings came and took our treasure. The English came and took our culture. During the Dark Ages, Ireland was the light of the world. Scholars came from Europe to study in our monasteries. Our monks copied and preserved the Word of God and the works of man. The world looked to Ireland to save civilization. There were hundreds of monasteries in Ireland. All schools of prayer and learning."

He stomped his staff on the ground and said in an angry voice that scared me. "Cromwell came and what he did not destroy, King Henry VIII suppressed."

His voice softened. "So here we are, I travel from one ruined monastery to another and you," he touched my cheek, "what would you become if you had a school to go to?" His eyes seemed filled with sadness. "Without schools, how can we make scholars?" He shook his head. "Now we are the ones in the Dark Ages."

I wondered if my eyes reflected his sadness. He stroked my cheek and said, "It's not your fault, my son."

CHAPTER 44

The light was fading in the forest. Brother Brendan picked up his pace. There was no time to think upon his words. I had to struggle to keep up with him. I carried the seaweed on my shoulder and clutched the bag of mushrooms to my chest. I couldn't match his longer stride and when I'd fall behind, I'd have to run to catch up to him.

The path took us out of the forest to the road. I looked around and breathed a sigh of relief. I knew where I was and even in the dark I could find my way home. I stood on the road and looked back at the darkening path to the forest. I'd walked past this path so many times and never knew where it led.

When we came to the crossroads, I stopped.

"My home is down this way," I said.

Brother Brendan looked down the road.

Rather than think it through, I just blurted out, "It's almost dark. Why don't you come home with me? You can spend the night and continue your pilgrimage in the morning."

"No, I must go on."

"But it'll be dark soon."

"I have no fear of the dark. I walk in the light of the Lord."

I handed the bag of mushrooms to him, but he pushed them back to me.

"Share them with your family." He stepped forward and placed his hand on my shoulder. "Hard times are upon us and I fear they will get worse. We must be men of faith."

He raised his right hand and I knelt in front of him.

"Under what name were you baptized?"

"Daniel," I replied.

"It is a strong name. Do you know its meaning?"

I shook my head.

"God is my judge." He traced his fingers across my forehead. "Be strong Daniel and trust in Our Lord."

He helped me to my feet. He looked into my eyes and I felt like he was trying to see my future. He said in a solemn voice, "I will pray to the Lord to give you strength."

I met his serious gaze and then lowered my head.

We parted at the crossroads. He went one way and I another. I wondered if our paths would ever cross again.

CHAPTER 45

Some days it rained, but you could feel the sun above the clouds. Other days it rained and it felt like the sun deserted us.

It was a cold rain and a dreary day. I had gotten to the crossroads first. The line of people who waited for the soup cart stood restlessly behind me. As we waited longer and longer the frustration turned to fear. It rained harder. Water rolled off my cap and snuck down my collar.

Hours passed. I knew in my heart that the cart wasn't coming.

A woman lamented, "What are we to do?"

Because of the rain, I couldn't tell if some of the Irish were crying. One person left and then another. They shuffled off with their heads down. Their arms clutched their empty stomachs.

I was the first in line and the last to leave.

My Ma and sisters waited in the cottage. I came through the doorway empty-handed. My Ma didn't have to say anything. Her face said it all. I hung up my wet cap and coat. I went and sat by the fire.

The next morning, I lay in my bed. I tried to catch the dream that was fleeing. In my dream, my Ma sang as she stirred a pot of potatoes over the fire. My Da and Paddy sat at the table. They laughed as they shared a story. My sisters walked into the cottage with a bucket of Millie's milk. Michael's warm breath was on my neck as he snuggled against me. I turned to him and the dream vanished.

In the darkness of our cottage, I sat on the edge of my bed and cradled my head between my hands. I sat like that until the sun rose.

I knew there was no reason to go to the crossroads. There'd be no soup coming. We couldn't wait for my Da any longer. The oats were ready to harvest. We couldn't afford to lose them. I got up from my bed and sat at the table next to my empty bowl. My Ma stood by the fire. She boiled some rice she had hidden away.

I said to my Ma, "We can't wait for Da. We have to start the harvest. Gale Day is coming. We have no money to pay the rent."

"Your Da will be here to help with the harvest."

I felt like smashing the table. It wasn't a time for hope. It was a time to do. I grabbed the scythe that was propped against the wall on the other side of the hearth. I carried it out the doorway.

The field of oats was golden in the sunshine. The wind swayed the tops of the amber grain. Next to the grain was the black graveyard of our potatoes. I couldn't understand why the grain thrived while our potatoes died.

I felt so small as I looked out to the field. The scythe was heavy in my hands. Always before, my Da and Paddy would do the cutting while I just gathered the fallen oats. I'd never cut before, but I watched them plenty of times. I lifted the scythe. I hoped I wouldn't cut myself.

It seemed like I only made a small dent into the field. My arms ached. I rested and looked behind me. My Ma and sisters were gathering our oats.

CHAPTER 46

The wind howled and rain pelted the thatch above my head. I couldn't sleep and I don't think anyone else could. We were all in our beds trying to stay warm. The dying embers were just a glow in the hearth. I thought about putting another cut of peat on the fire, but that meant I'd have to get out from under the covers and walk across the cold floor.

The door crashed open. In the dim light, I saw a dark shape come into our cottage. I sprang to my feet. My heart pounded. The figured turned and shut the door. I stood frozen with fear. The dark shape moved across our cottage to the hearth. It bent and tossed a cut of peat on the fire. In the dim light, the dark figure took the shape of a man. The man walked and collapsed onto the chair set before the hearth.

I knew my Da was home.

My Ma helped my Da take off his coat. She dried his face with a towel and wrapped a blanket around his shoulders. I sat by the fire and stared at him. He seemed so much older than I remembered. His unruly hair and beard were streaked with gray. His face was the color of ashes. He coughed and then coughed again and again. It was a cough that seemed to come from deep in his chest. My Ma brought him a mug of water. He pushed her hand away. He bent and coughed and coughed into his fist. He wheezed as he gasped for air between the coughs.

Finally, the spasm ended. I watched the rise and fall of my Da's chest. My Ma came forward and offered the mug again. This time he took it. His hand shook as he brought the mug to his mouth and drank. I stared at the blood caked on his hand. I barely noticed the water that dripped into his beard.

My Ma wouldn't let me or my sisters come near my Da. She boiled oatmeal and fed him one small spoonful and then another. He choked and coughed up more than he ate. She helped him to his feet and struggled with him to their bed. I wanted to help, but she shooed me away.

It was hours until dawn. We all tried to go back to bed, but as soon as I'd drift off to sleep, the coughing would start again.

Black rain clouds stayed on top of our cottage. We piled peat on the fire to chase the chill away. My Da would come awake with his cough spasms and then drift back to sleep when they passed. When he finally awoke my Ma bathed him with a bucket of warm water from the fire.

My Ma cooked a pot of oatmeal. It wasn't as tasty with no milk or butter, but it filled me much better than soup. She tried to feed a small portion of oatmeal to my Da, but he just pushed her hand away. There were beads of sweat on his brow as if he were working in the sunshine. His brown eyes seemed afire. My ma looked at me. I saw the fear in her eyes. I didn't know what to do.

A hard spasm rocked my Da's chest. His face contorted and I felt his pain. His hand came away from his mouth covered with blood. My Ma washed his hand with a wet cloth and bathed his face.

I never felt more helpless.

My Da pointed and said in a weak, hoarse voice, "My coat."

I quickly crossed the room and brought his coat to him. His fingers fumbled with the pocket. He brought out his coin pouch. He looked at me and placed the pouch in my hand. It was heavy with the coins he must have earned in England.

He coughed and blood bubbled on his lips. My Ma wiped his mouth. My Da closed his eyes and drifted back to sleep. I stood by his bed with the pouch of coins in my hand. I had never been so scared in my life.

Night came. My Ma wouldn't leave my Da's bedside. My sisters prayed. I wished that Brother Brendan were here. He would know what to do.

My Da's coughs grew weaker. When he breathed, he sounded like he was bubbling water. His breaths became shallower.

I cried because there was nothing I could do.

Hours passed and then my Da suddenly gasped. His body went rigid and then still. His open eyes were fixed on my Ma's face.

My Ma screamed and threw her arms around him as if she could stop him from leaving.

My sisters screamed.

I collapsed to the floor and sobbed.

CHAPTER 47

We buried my Da on my 12th birthday.

The wind carried my family's wailings for miles, but our neighbors didn't come. It wasn't the Ireland of time gone by. My Da had no grand wake with friends and family who'd tell stories of his greatness. We lived in a time of too many sorrows to be shared.

I didn't know how to make a coffin. I knew no one I could ask for help. We wrapped my Da in his bedsheets that were stained with his own blood. My Ma and I carried him to the place where his father and grandfather were buried on the land that we once owned. I dug a deep grave. I didn't want the animals to disturb his slumber. We returned him gently to the earth that he farmed. My sisters weaved a St. Brigid's Cross of straw and placed it on his grave.

My Ma was all cried out. I so wished Thomas and Sarah were here. Sarah could help my Ma in ways that I could not. My sisters led my Ma back to our cottage. I stood by my Da's grave. I thought of the pouch of coins that he gave me. I knew he gave me so much more.

I didn't know how we could survive. I had so much to learn and now he was not here to teach me. I sat beside his grave numb with grief. Twilight came among us. I knew what my Da wanted. I couldn't leave until I fulfilled his need.

I stood. The words came soft. I sang the song of parting.
The song that always made my Da cry,

> "*The Minstrel fell! But the foeman's chain*
> *Could not bring that proud soul under;*
> *The harp he lov'd ne'er spoke again,*
> *For he tore its chords asunder;*
> *And said, "No chains shall sully thee,*
> *Thou soul of love and brav'ry!*
> *Thy songs were made for the pure and free,*
> *They shall never sound in slavery!"*

CHAPTER 48

We had no choice. We had to finish our harvest. We needed the oats to pay the rent. Once the rent was paid, the money my Da brought home from England would hopefully see us through the winter.

The hard work was a blessing. My Ma left her tears inside the cottage. She came out to the field and helped us. She worked by our side, but she was never the same after my Da died. I think part of her died with him.

It was a bumper harvest. No matter what, I wouldn't give it all to Coghlan. With Millie and our pig gone, the small cottage that held our livestock was empty. I waited until the sun went down and under the cover of darkness, I snuck out and hid some of our bundled oats behind the straw in the cottage. I figured it wasn't stealing. It was rightfully ours.

At the breakfast table, I heard the rumble of carts. I grabbed my coat and cap and rushed outside. Coghlan rode his horse down the lane to our cottage. A line of carts followed him. He stopped and turned to his men and waved his hand. His laborers climbed down from the carts and walked into the field to gather our grain that was cut and bundled.

He rode up to me. His black horse pawed the earth. I tried to be brave and meet his stare, but he always made me feel like a child.

"Where's you Da?" he asked.

He had to know. Nothing happened in our hamlet that he didn't know.

I pointed to the hillside. "He's over there, buried by his father and grandfather."

He stared down at me from his horse. We both knew my Da wasn't here to protect me. I cringed under his intense gaze. I wondered what thoughts were in his mind.

My Ma and sisters came out of our cottage and stood behind me.

I tried to say in a strong voice, but my words still sounded like a child's. "You have our oats. The rent is paid."

He laughed. He mimicked my boyish voice, "The rent is paid."

He edged his horse closer to me. He leaned over and said, "We both know it's just a matter of time."

I stepped back. I felt my Ma's hand rest protectively on my shoulder.

Coghlan yanked the reins. He spurred his horse and rode out to our fields.

CHAPTER 49

Our clachan was destroyed. Coghlan tumbled Sarah and Thomas' cottage first.

We stood in front of our home and watched from a distance. Coghlan arrived with his men. The Sheriff came with a handful of soldiers. There was no need for the soldiers at Thomas' cottage. There was no one to try and stop them.

The Sheriff walked to the cottage. He tore off the "notice to quit" that he had previously posted on the door. He pounded on the door and then walked into the empty cottage. He came out and talked with Coghlan. They argued. I don't know about what. The Sheriff left and took the soldiers with him to go to the next cottage.

I expected Coghlan to send his men into the cottage to take Thomas' possessions and toss them to the yard, but he didn't. Coghlan barked an order. His men took crowbars to the stones. When the walls weakened, they tied a rope to the rafters. They gave the rope to Coghlan who tied it to his saddle. He eased his horse forward. The roof and walls tumbled.

My Ma continuously squeezed one hand with the other. We watched as a cottage that sheltered generations for ages was destroyed in a few minutes. The men took a torch to the thatch. Dark smoke billowed to the sky.

Coghlan turned his horse toward our cottage. I felt his gaze upon me. He was too far away. I couldn't see his face. But I didn't have to. I knew the stare he was giving me.

Coghlan rode from Thomas' cottage to our village. His men followed him and I followed the men.

I knew some of the cottages in our clachan, like Thomas', were already abandoned. All it took for some families to abandon a cottage was the Sheriff's notice on the door that the rent was overdue. Men who didn't have money to pay the rent knew they could be sent to jail. Without the husband, the family stood little chance of survival. The husbands felt they had no choice but to pack up their meager belongings and abandon their homes. The family would stay together. They would take their chances on the road. They became part of the wanderers.

Those who stayed were evicted.

Coghlan wasn't interested in sending anyone to jail. He just wanted the farmers gone. If the family didn't have money for the rent, the walls came down. The Sheriff gave the families little time to gather their few things of value. Mothers and children, who clung to their aprons, sobbed. The mothers beseeched Coghlan to let them stay. Coghlan was a hard man. He ignored their heartbreaking pleas as he went about his business. Fathers who opposed him were pushed aside by the soldiers. Coghlan went from one cottage to another. The walls came down. Rising smoke could be seen for miles.

It was a day of unbelievable sadness. In one day Carrigillihy disappeared.

For Coghlan, it wasn't enough to have destroyed the cottages, the farmers must be gone. He sat on his horse and waited while the soldiers herded the farmers together and drove them down the road.

CHAPTER 50

The next morning my Ma sat at our kitchen table and stared vacantly at the fire. She seemed like a statue. It was left for my sisters to make our breakfast. My Ma wouldn't touch her oatmeal. I had never been as worried about her as I was that morning. I felt like my Ma's body was there, but her mind wasn't. I wished she would pray, at least then I'd know she was still with us. She sat like that for hours. When she finally did get up, she walked to the bed she shared with my Da. She got in the bed and turned to the wall. She didn't move for the rest of the day.

Mary and Joanna took turns sitting by her. Our home was deathly quiet. I couldn't bear to sit and do nothing. I had to get out of the cottage.

I searched the rubble of Sarah and Thomas' cottage. What wasn't broken was consumed by the fire. There were some metal pots and utensils that survived. We didn't need them, but I thought I could take them to the pawn shop in Skibbereen.

I walked among the ruins and thought about all the people who had lived in this cottage: so many families over so many years. All that was left to mark their passage were the pot and forks I held in my hand.

I sat on top of the stones amid the ruins. The wind came from the ocean. It was a cold wind. I gathered my coat around me. Winter would soon be upon us. I stared across the field to our cottage. Smoke rose from our chimney and was whisked away by the wind. The sadness came upon me. I knew it was just a matter of time. Someday our cottage would be tumbled like the others and cows would graze upon the ruins of our lives.

CHAPTER 51

My Ma stayed in her bed. There were too many sorrows for her to bear all at once, Time passed slowly in our somber cottage.

I awoke one morning to find my Ma cooking oatmeal in our pot above the peat. I sat at the table and she brought me my oatmeal. She never talked about the time of her sadness. I never asked. I was just happy to have her back.

Such as it was our life went on. One day blended into another. We lived off the oatmeal I had hidden away. When the weather was fair, I'd go to the ocean to gather seaweed while my Ma and sisters would search for roots.

The cold north wind came again as it did last winter and drove us inside. My sisters bickered as only sisters who spend too much time together can. There were days I'd face the cold outside to get away from their whining.

December came and with it came Christmas. My Ma said we would go to Christmas Mass. My sisters didn't want to go, but my Ma was adamant. Mary and Joanna cried that they had nothing fit to wear to church. My Ma snapped back, "Do you think anyone else does?" Her words silenced my sisters. My Ma boiled a pot of water above the peat. She sent me outside as they washed.

It snowed the night before. I opened our cottage's door. Gleaming light reflected off fresh snow that was so bright it hurt my eyes. It was cold, but it was one of our few days with no wind so it didn't feel so cold. I gathered my coat and cap and went out into the brightness. As far as I could see everything was covered by a beautiful white veil. It felt so good to see the sun. I breathed in. The cold air filled my lungs. It was the type of day that held promise.

We went to St. Patrick's Church early. My Ma wanted to pray her rosary before Mass. She said she had a lot of souls to pray for, both living and dead. Mary and Joanna were sullen on our walk to the church. Other Irish met us on the road. My sisters wouldn't meet anyone's eyes. They were dressed better than most of the Irish farmers we met on our way to church. They were cleaner.

When we got to town, I understood how my sisters felt. The town women, especially the young women, were dressed in their finery. With their long warm coats and gloves, they walked with their heads held high. Their rosy cheeks glowed. Their eyes were bright. Their hair was neatly arranged beneath their hats. It wasn't that they shunned us, but we walked around them just the same.

The townsfolk sat near the altar. We got there early enough to get a pew toward the back of the church. It wasn't long before all the pews were full and people stood against the walls. The church warmed and filled with the smell of humanity.

Christmas Mass began in all its splendor. I could speak and understand Gaelic and English. I knew the familiar cadence of the priest's Latin prayers, but as a boy, I didn't understand the words he said. As Mass went on, my eyes and mind drifted.

Some of the Irish were too weak to stand for the whole Mass. They slowly sank to the floor and then leaned back against the wall. One elderly woman was overcome. She collapsed. Luckily, those near her caught her as she fell.

As it grew warmer in church, incense couldn't mask the smell of the clothes and the unwashed bodies around us. I think it made it worse. I watched as the weak helped the weaker to shuffle forward to receive communion. I wondered if the Good Lord's bread would nourish our bodies as much as our souls.

The Mass ended and that's when our real Christmas began.

Chapter 52

When Mass was over, Father said the good people of Skibbereen invited us all to go to the old Steam Mill to share a Christmas meal. I looked to my Ma. She smiled and nodded. Even my sisters seemed happy.

The old Steam Mill was the building where they had the soup kitchen before the British decided to shut all the soup kitchens down. We walked into the cavernous room. I breathed in the air. I couldn't believe the smell. The room was filled with the aroma of roasting meat. The smell set my mouth to watering.

We sat on the same benches that we had used when we came to the soup kitchen. They gave us bowls full of porridge that was so thick it clung to my spoon. I savored the taste of butter and milk. When we finished the porridge, I wondered if my eyes grew as big as my sisters' when they brought out platters of ham and beef and bread still warm from the ovens.

No one talked as we ate. It was as if each person went into their own private world. I looked around our table. My sisters cried as they chewed the meat.

I tried to eat slowly to savor each bite. It had been so long since I had meat, I almost forgot its taste. I found myself crying with the others.

I wanted to eat more, but I couldn't. My stomach had quickly filled. I was surprised, because I didn't really eat that much. I thought maybe there was something the matter with my stomach. Maybe it had shrunk from never having enough food.

They started to take the platters away. The man across from me snuck his hand along the table. He snatched a piece of ham and hid it in his pocket. He looked across at me. He knew I saw what he did. He smiled and motioned for me to do the same. And I did.

They cleared the tables and brought out tea and desserts. My stomach was full, but that didn't matter. I would find room for a piece of cake.

I looked at the people who gave us food. I knew they were Irish like us, but I felt they were different. I wondered if you lived in a town, if that made you different.

I recognized one of the women who brought out the cakes. She and her husband were the ones who drove the soup cart out to our clachan. I remembered her name was Mary, like my sister's. She was beautiful, all prim and proper. I wanted to go up and thank her, but I was embarrassed. I understood how my sisters felt. If I went up to her in my clothes that were no better than rags, what would she think of me?

No one was in a hurry to leave. We sat with our hands resting on our full stomachs in the warmth of the kitchen. People talked. There were even some smiles. It had been so long since I had seen the Irish smile.

I looked around the room. The tables were all full, but then it struck me there was no one waiting to sit. When we came here for the soup, there were people waiting in a line as far as I could see. What happened to all those people? Where did they go?

Our Christmas wasn't over. There was another large room next to the kitchen. In the room, there were tables piled with clothes. Father said the Catholic Churches in New York took up donations and shipped them to us across the ocean. He said each of us could take one piece that we felt we needed most. My sisters wandered off like they were in a candy shop.

My Ma took my hand. She knew what she wanted. There was a section of boys' clothes. She ignored the pants and shirts, scarves and mittens. She wanted a coat for me. She found one that was too big, but she said I would grow. The coat was coarse and thick. I knew it wasn't new. There were some stains and stitches that mended rips. I tried it on. It was warm. I thought some boy in America had worn this coat. I wondered what his life was like. I thought of Paddy and Michael.

My Ma spun me around to take a good look. The next thing I knew she hugged me. Even through the coat, I could feel her frail body. She stepped back and we looked at each other. Her hair was streaked with white. Her brown eyes seemed like they sunk into her pale face. There were creases on her forehead and wrinkles around her eyes. I wondered when she grew so old. I wondered what she saw when she looked at me.

The sun was still shining as we left the old Steam Mill. I wore my new coat. I felt like a different person. We walked down the street. There were Irish gathered outside one of the shops. I knew it was the pawnshop. I slid my hands into my coat's pockets. I didn't want to look at the people waiting outside of the shop. I knew what they were going to do. They would pawn their gift of clothes so that they would have money to buy food for tomorrow.

CHAPTER 53

Winter passed slowly. The oats I had hidden away were long gone. The money that my Da had earned in England was all but spent.

I'd wake up in the middle of the night. I couldn't go back to sleep. We had no money left to buy food. We had no seed potatoes or grain to plant. I'd lie awake and worry about what would happen to us when the rent came due.

The days lengthened and the weather warmed. I thought if we could just stay in our cottage until the summer, we could live off the land. There'd be berries for the picking and seaweed from the ocean. There'd be turnips and onions and cabbages. If we could stay in our cabin we could make it through the summer and part of the fall. The winter...I wouldn't think about.

But Gale Day would come before summer and our food was all but gone.

I told myself it was getting warm enough that I didn't need my coat. It was a long walk to the pawnshop and a longer walk home. The few pence I got for my coat were barely enough to buy a small bag of grain. The merchant felt sorry for me. He gave me a loaf of bread. I tried to save some of the bread for my Ma and sisters, but it was a long walk home and I was so hungry.

From the road, I could see our cabin's door was closed. It was strange because we always left it open in the daytime. As I got closer, I saw the paper on the door. I couldn't read it, but I didn't have to. I'd seen the same paper posted before on other doors.

We had our "notice to quit."

I entered our home. My Ma knelt by the fire. She prayed her rosary. My sisters were in their bed. They held each other and cried.

CHAPTER 54

I couldn't sleep. I got out of bed and left our cottage. I walked under a canopy of stars. I shivered without my coat. Dew clung to the fields. The shadows of the dead returned to the earth as the sun rose. I walked to Lord Townsend's estate. I had no choice. I had to see Coghlan.

I saw him from afar. The wall around Lord Townsend's Manor House was almost finished. Coghlan sat on his horse and watched the men who sacked stones higher than their heads. I had no doubt that he was waiting for me. I knew he saw me, but he didn't ride out to meet me. He would make me come to him. As I got closer to him, he turned his horse. He left the workers and rode to the Manor House. I followed.

He rode past the gardens. Buds from the flowers started to peek from the earth. The Manor House loomed stately and quiet. He rode to the stable and dismounted. A new boy came out of the stable. He was younger than Timothy, the stable boy I saw before.

Coghlan said in a cold, hard voice, "What do you want?"

Fear seized me. It was all I could do not to turn and run away. I was ashamed of my voice as I squeaked, "I need a job."

"It's too late for that. You had your chance." He motioned to the boy who led his horse to the stable. "That job's been taken."

"I'll work hard. I'll do what you ask."

He walked up and stared down at me. I don't know what went through his mind, but his face changed.

"Let's see if you will." He pushed me toward the stable. Away from the door's light, the stable was in shadows. He shouted to the stable boy, "Take my horse out to the field and let him graze."

The boy led the horse away. I knew we were alone. Coghlan walked toward me.

"I'll do what you ask." I backed away and lifted my hands. "But you must let my Ma and sisters stay in the cabin."

He pushed me. I crashed into the wall behind me. "Your cabin and family are gone. I'll not change that." He grabbed the front of my shirt. The shirt ripped as he lifted me up on my toes. "You can sleep in the stable. You'll have food to eat. That's all that I offer."

"No. You must let my family stay."

His hand moved so fast. The back of his knuckle split my cheek as he slapped me. I fell to the ground. He kicked me. I rolled. He was upon me. His harsh breath felt like it burned my ear. One hand lifted me by my collar as his other hand grabbed my pants.

The anger came upon me. I lashed out. I kicked. I punched. He threw me to the ground. I scrambled to my feet. He backed away. His hand disappeared into his coat. I charged. He brought the pistol from his pocket and fired.

I froze. My ears rang. I stared at the pistol's two barrels that he pointed at my face. He cocked the lever for the second barrel. Behind the pistol, his chest heaved. So did mine. Smoke drifted up to his face. His eyes burned with more than hatred.

CHAPTER 55

The hand that held the pistol was steady. I wondered if he'd kill me. I lowered my fists and stood there and waited.

I heard voices outside. The shot had alarmed them.

He uncocked the pistol and motioned with it. "Go home while you still have a home to go to."

The anger still burned inside me. I stared at him. I don't know for how long. He stood between me and the door. I walked up to and then around him. I didn't look back. He laughed as I left. It was the laugh of the devil.

I walked through the fields. My cheek was on fire. I don't know if the burning was from his hand or his pistol. I held my hand to my cheek to try and stem the blood that ran down my fingers.

I stopped at the creek and washed the blood from my face and hand. I felt the bone beneath the gash in my skin. I sat and leaned back against the bank. I tried to press and hold the split flesh together. My right ear still rang with the gunshot. The smell rose from me. I don't know if the stink was fear or anger. All of a sudden, I was so tired. I didn't know if I had the strength to get up. The cold came from within me. I started to shake. I turned to my side. My right hand cupped my cheek. I brought my knees to my chest. My body shook, but I was so tired.

I drifted to sleep.

CHAPTER 56

We knew it was just a matter of time. There was nothing that we could do to stop them from coming. My Ma wanted me to pray the rosary with her, but I couldn't. I believed in the devil. I wasn't so sure about God.

I sat in my Da's chair by the fire. I wondered, if he were here, what he would do. I had no answer. My cheek throbbed. It was hot to the touch. I felt empty inside.

We heard the rumble of the cart on the lane. There was a loud knock on the door. I'll never forget the look of terror on my Ma's face. My sisters ran to her. They held each other. My Ma wailed. It was a piercing keening that broke my heart. They clung to each and keened.

The door sprang open and Coghlan walked in. I ran to my Ma. Coghlan took a quick look around. His face was all business.

He shouted, "Get her out!"

My Ma stopped her wailing. Her eyes were red. Her chin quivered as she held her hands out beseechingly to Coghlan.

He gave her a look of disgust.

He said to me, "Get her out of here, now!"

I took hold of one of my Ma's arms. Mary took hold of the other. We led my Ma from her home.

The Sheriff was outside with Coghlan's men and their crowbars. There were no soldiers. Coghlan knew he didn't need them. My Da and brothers were gone. The neighbors were gone. I was all that was left. Coghlan had no fear of me.

There was nothing to take from our cottage. Anything of value that we had, we had either pawned or bartered for food. All we had left were the clothes that we wore.

We stood in front of our cottage like prisoners and watched the destruction of our lives. It was quick work. Coghlan's men already had a lot of practice. The walls came down. A worker set a torch to the thatch. The Sheriff stood off to the side. His face was as glum as mine.

Coghlan pulled papers from his coat pocket and walked to the Sheriff.

"They're paupers now," he said. "Take them to the workhouse."

My Ma screamed. She sank to the ground and pulled me down with her. Behind Coghlan, the thatch burned fiercely like the fires of hell. My Ma lifted her hand as if she could ward off his words.

Coghlan pushed the papers into the Sheriff's hands. "Their papers are all signed." He turned to his men. "We're done here. Get back in the cart." He walked and mounted his horse. He reined his dark steed toward me.

My Ma clutched her hands to her chest. She rocked back and forth. Her wails subsided to moans.

Coghlan towered over us. He stared at my face. I wouldn't turn my scared cheek from him. He gave me such a wicked grin. He knew that he had won. Our land was now his. He would have his pasture.

He looked out to our fields. I expected a howl of triumph. He pulled the reins to his chest and spurred his horse. He left without a backward glance.

He rode away, but not out of my life.

CHAPTER 57

The Sheriff walked to his horse. He took the reins and led his horse to us. He stood and waited.

I went and stared at the dying fire. Our home was gone and with it the life we knew. I wanted to run. I knew the workhouse was no place for me. Soon it would be warm enough that I could live off the land. If I ran, I didn't think the Sheriff would try and stop me. I knew by myself I could survive, but what of my family? I'd have to leave my Ma and sisters.

My Ma sat on the ground and looked beyond pitiful. I felt her sadness. She cried softly into her rosary that she held by her mouth. Joanna sat next to her. She was like my Ma. She couldn't bear the sadness. Mary stood behind them. She wasn't sad. She was angry. She and I were like our Da.

The Sheriff said, "It's time to go."

The urge to run almost set my feet in motion. I knew no good would come from the workhouse. My Ma looked up at me. I always thought she was so strong, but now she seemed so helpless. I knew in my heart that I couldn't leave her. I went to my Ma and took her arm and helped her to her feet. Mary helped our sister.

The Sheriff mounted his horse and led us to the workhouse.

The workhouse was set on a hill. You could see it for miles. It was the largest building in my childhood. Its high stone walls made it seem like a fortress or a prison. I didn't know if it was designed to keep people in or out.

The workhouse wasn't that old. It was built when I was a child. We'd see the monstrosity take shape when we walked down the road to Skibbereen. I never knew anyone who went there by choice. When it opened, the only people who would go there were the dying who were penniless. They went for the coffin and the Christian burial they'd be given at the workhouse.

The road to the workhouse was lined with misery. Irish collapsed by the roadside. They only had the strength to go so far up the hill and then no farther. Off to the side of the road, people lay on the berm of the ditch. They didn't move when we walked by. Flies buzzed above them.

I couldn't believe my eyes. There had to be hundreds if not thousands of people gathered outside of the gates to the workhouse. More people than I could ever count. Their bodies were skeletons and their eyes were vacant. I didn't see many young children or old folks. We followed the Sheriff as his horse pushed its way through the horde of starving humanity. People had their hands out as we walked by. They lowered their hands when they realized we were no better than them.

At the gatehouse, the Sheriff wouldn't get down from his horse. He took the papers from his coat and gave them to the gatekeeper. I didn't know if the papers that gave us the right to enter the workhouse were a blessing or a curse. We were allowed to enter while hundreds of others were denied. I helped my Ma while Mary helped Joanna. The Sheriff kept the starving Irish from entering behind us.

The gate closed and my life changed once again.

CHAPTER 58

The door closed behind us and we were separated from the mayhem outside. It was much quieter in the admissions area. We walked to an office where a middle-age man sat behind a large wooden desk. He wore glasses, a dark coat, and a white starched shirt. He looked haggard and beyond himself. He barely gave us a glance as he took our papers and studied them. Finally, he signed them and tossed them on an overflowing pile. He flicked his hand. We walked from the office area.

The admission room was white and barren. The Matron of the workhouse stood there to greet us. She was a large woman. She was so different from us. She was clean and healthy. Her clothes were spotless. She eyed us and walked around us, but she wouldn't come close.

In an exacting voice, she asked my Ma, "How old is the boy?"

My ma opened her mouth, but no words came out.

"I'm 12," I said.

"You look too tall for 12. We have some men come in here and say they're younger so that they can stay with boys instead of men. At 15, a boy's a man here.

"I'm 12."

The Matron faced my sisters. "And the girls?"

Mary spoke up and said, "I'm 16."

The matron turned to Joanna. My sister looked stricken. She blurted, "I'm…"

Mary cut in and said loudly, "Joanna's 15. We were born 10 months apart, but in the same year."

I knew what Mary was doing. Joanna was only 14.

The Matron shook her head as if she didn't believe Mary.

My Ma gathered her senses. "It's true. They came one after the other. They both took my milk at the same time."

The Matron shrugged her wide shoulders as if it was no concern of hers. She said to me, "Say your goodbyes, now." She motioned to the exit. "Once through the door, men and women, boys and girls stay separate."

"My Ma said, "We're family. Surely, I'll see my boy."

"You won't."

My Ma reeled like she was slapped.

I saw the coldness in the Matron's eyes. She stood back and waited.

I went to my Ma. Her tears flowed and she started to shake. She was hunched over. I was as tall as her. I gathered my arms around her. I could feel the bones of her spine. Her tears wet my cheeks. My sisters gathered around. Our arms entwined.

I fought the tears. I didn't want to cry in front of the Matron. It was too much. I couldn't take the sadness anymore. I pushed myself away and walked backwards from my family.

My Ma held out her rosary and cried, "I'll pray for you."

She seemed so small and weak and frightened. I mouthed the words, "I love you."

The Matron moved toward me. I backed away to the door with my eyes still filled with the vision of my mother.

That was the last time I saw my Ma.

CHAPTER 59

I backed out of the doorway. The Matron followed. She froze me with her stare. She called out, "Johnnie."

A boy, who looked not much older than me, stuck his head out of a room down the hallway. He saw the Matron and quickly walked to us. I couldn't help but to stare at the boy. A blemish covered half his face from his forehead to his chin. The stain was dark red - almost purple. I'd never seen the likes of it before. His hair was cut short and he had jug ears that stood out from the sides of his head. He had a small jaw and there seemed to be too many teeth in his mouth.

The Matron said, "Take him and show him where he will stay." She huffed and added, "He's half naked. See if you can find some clothes that are better than his rags." She turned abruptly and went back to my family.

The boy was only slightly taller than me. He seemed as serious as the Matron. He yanked my arm and said, "Come on."

He pulled me down the hallway and then led me into a side room. Clothes were piled atop wooden tables. He looked around. There was no one there but us. He caught me staring at his face. I didn't look away and neither did he.

"Does it hurt?" I asked.

He looked like he was confused by my question.

He slowly shook his head and said, "I was born this way. It's just skin like yours." He rubbed his cheek. "It's just a different color."

I wanted to touch his face, but I didn't. I nodded that I understood.

He asked, "What happened to your face?"

"A man hit me."

It was his turn to nod that he understood. The seriousness seemed to leave him and he looked at me not unkindly.

"What's your name?"

"It's Danny."

I looked behind him to the bundles of clothes. I walked toward the nearest bunch. As I got closer, I saw the clothes were rags no better than mine.

"No. Not those," Johnnie said. He cut in front of me and pushed me away. "Those are dead boys' clothes. Those boys died from the fever." He looked at the rags with revulsion. "No luck will come from wearing those. If it was up to me, I burn them. Over here."

He walked to a far table in the back of the room. He dug through a pile of clean clothes and pulled out a shirt. He held it up in front of me. "That should fit."

I felt the coarse material. It looked like the same shirt that Johnnie wore under his coat.

Johnnie continued his search. "Before the famine, these clothes are what they used to give the paupers to wear. But now, there're too many paupers and not enough clothes so we don't give them out anymore." He found a pair of pants. He held them up in front of him and then tossed them to me.

I wondered why he was being kind to me.

"You'll need a coat."

I started to take off my filthy, tattered shirt as he searched through the clothes.

He looked up and saw what I was doing.

"No. Not here." He shook his head. "You stink. If you're going to wear clean clothes, you need to wash first."

I felt like a fool.

Johnnie finally found a coat. He handed it to me. I gathered it in my arms with the other clothes.

He glanced at my bare feet that were so dirty that they looked darker than peat.

"You'll feel right at home. Boys don't wear shoes here. Come on, let's get you a bath."

CHAPTER 60

Johnnie took me to the baths. I hadn't bathed since Christmas. I pulled off my shirt and pants. It felt like part of my skin peeled away as I unstuck my underclothes. I dropped the clothes I had lived in for months in a heap by my feet. The man who worked the baths came at me with scissors. I didn't know what he was going to do. I stood there naked. I brought my hands up to fight.

"It's OK, Danny," said Johnnie. "He's just going to cut your hair."

I lowered my hands and tried to cover my nakedness as best as I could. The man roughly grabbed a clump of my hair and started to cut. He tossed the shorn hair on my clothes.

The man was all business. He finished my hair and set down the scissors. He picked up a bar of soap and tossed it to me. He grabbed a bucket of water and dumped it over my head. I shivered like a duck. Johnnie stood off to the side and laughed. The man told me to scrub myself. I scrubbed as best as I could.

Another bucket of water was poured over my head. My skin stung and turned bright red. I dried and put on the clothes that Johnnie gave me. They were rough, but clean. The pants were too long and the shirt too tight, but they were so much better than the rotten shreds gathered by my ankles.

Johnnie led me down the long hallway. The hallway was
cold and damp. The walls were stark and white. You could
see the wooden beams in the ceiling. The floor wasn't wood or
stones, but it was too hard to be just earth. I don't know what
it was.

At the end of the hallway was a large wooden door that was
closed. Johnnie slowly pulled open the door. I thought the
room had to be empty because the room was so quiet. I was
amazed that there were hundreds of boys inside. The boys were
squeezed tight together, elbow to elbow, as they sat at the
benches of the long wooden tables where they ate their meals.
I wondered why no one talked. The boys all stared at us as we
entered. A few wore the workhouse garb like I wore, but most
of the boys wore the clothes they had on when they came to
the workhouse. The room was warm and filled with the smell
of boys. Every table was full with boys about my age or older. I
wondered where the younger boys where.

"I got to get back," Johnnie said. "Find a place to sit and
get some food. Just follow the others when they leave."

He turned and walked away. The door closed behind him.
I stood not knowing what to do. I swallowed my sudden fear.
I was in a roomful of strangers. The boys went back to eating.
Spoons scraped along the bottom of empty bowls.

On the other side of the room was the main table where two
young men ladled oatmeal into bowls. I walked to the table
and took a bowl of stirabout and a spoon. I was so hungry, I
wanted to eat the oatmeal right where I stood, but I didn't. I
took a mug of water and searched for a spot to sit.

A boy got up to take his empty bowl back. I walked to his
place, but the empty spot disappeared before I got to it. The
boys had shifted on the bench and the opening vanished.

I wasn't to be denied. I squeezed in where the boy had sat. The boys on the bench next to me resisted, but it didn't come to a fight. They took a look at the cut on my face and let me be. I stared back at them until they looked away.

I inhaled my food. It was gone in seconds. The little food in my stomach only made me hungrier.

I wanted to ask if I could get more oatmeal, but no one talked at the table. So I stayed silent too.

It wasn't long until there was a silent signal that passed from one boy to the other. All the boys stood. I stood with them. We formed a line and left the dining room.

CHAPTER 61

The boys started to talk as soon as we left the dining room. The chatter was too much to take in all at once. We walked down another long hallway. The hallways seemed all the same. They were stark and white, cold and damp. Light came from the windows, but you couldn't see out. The bottom of the windows was higher than any boy's head.

The boys' steps slowed. They grew quiet as we came to another doorway. I didn't know what was behind the door, but I knew it was a place that the boys didn't want to go.

We entered an enormous room. Men were leaving through a doorway on the other side. In the center of the room, there was a contraption that I had never seen before. It was like a large wheel that lay on the ground. There were long poles that came out from the hub of the wheel. The boys reluctantly walked up to the wheel and grabbed ahold of the poles. There were four boys to each pole. I couldn't count how many poles there were around the wheel.

I did like the others. I walked up and put my hands on the pole and waited. There weren't enough places for all the boys. Those who didn't get a place went and sat and leaned back against the whitewashed wall. When the spots were all filled and everyone was ready, we started to push. It was hard to get going. We dug our toes into the floor. We pushed and pushed until the wheel slowly started to turn. We all moved together. We started to walk.

There was a loud grinding sound. I realized the wheel we pushed turned a stone that ground the grain that we would eat. I put one foot in front of the other. No one talked. Around and around and around we went. I lost all sense of time. My calves and fingers cramped. Weak boys grew tired and didn't push, but just walked behind the pole, which made it harder for the rest of us. The boy in front of me bent over his pole and threw up. No one stopped or seemed to notice. I had no choice but to walk through his vomit. We pushed on and on in an endless circle.

I didn't know how long it was until they called a break. There was a large bucket of water by the doorway. I went to get a drink with some of the others. Most boys were too tired to even walk to the water. They went to the nearest wall and slid down and sat. They hung their heads between their knees.

The ones who hadn't walked yet took our places at the wheel. There weren't enough of them. There were empty spots to be filled. They wouldn't start the walk again until all the spots were taken.

The tall boy who stood next to me took a gulp of water and tossed the rest on the floor. He walked and took an empty spot at the wheel. I looked at the boys who had collapsed by the wall. They didn't have the strength to go on. I still stood while they didn't. I went and took the empty place next to the tall boy.

"I'm, Aidan," the tall boy said.

I nodded to him and said, "Danny."

He was a good couple inches taller than me. His short hair was red as a robin's breast. There was red fuzz on his cheeks. His voice was much deeper than mine. He didn't have the pale face of the other boys, so I figured he must not have been here for too long.

Aidan put his hands on the pole and waited for the other spots to be filled. I looked at the boys gathered around me. Many of the boys were the ones who sat for the first turn of the wheel. I realized they did so for a reason. Some of them barely had the strength to stand.

When the spots were all finally filled, we started to push. Aidan was much stronger than me. I felt the pole start to move in my hands. I dug my toes and leaned my weight forward. The wheel slowly started to turn. Aidan pushed and I tried to match his strength. The wheel slowly turned. We pushed and walked. We pushed and walked.

I looked to the others. Some boys were so weak that they leaned on top of the pole so that the pole pulled them along.

Aidan noticed my stare and said to me, "If a boy doesn't walk, he's sent to the infirmary. There's fever among the sick. Boys who go there never come back."

His words chilled me.

"The strong carry the weak," Aidan said. "That's the way it is here. We do what we can for as long as we can."

I didn't want the burden he was giving me, but I knew I must accept it. I lowered my head and pushed the endless wheel.

CHAPTER 62

The wheel slowed and stopped, but I felt like I was still walking. My calves hurt like they never hurt before. It was a sharp pain, like someone stabbed needles into my legs. I fought the pain and went to the water bucket and drank.

"Come on," Aidan said. "Dinner's waiting."

His voice came from behind me. I turned to him and passed him the ladle. He dipped it in the bucket and took a drink. The boys formed a line by the door. Those that were too weak were supported by others.

"We do this every day?" I asked.

"Every day but Sunday."

I stared at the large wheel that now stood still. A sense of dread came over me. Aidan took my arm and pulled me along.

We fell silent as we entered the dining hall. I welcomed the quiet. I was too tired to talk or listen. Our dinner was soup and hard bread. I had better soup at the soup kitchen. The boy across from me broke open his bread. The inside was crawling with black weevils. He looked at me and shrugged. He took a piece of bread, dipped it in his soup, and shoved it in his mouth. I watched his face as he chewed and swallowed.

I steeled myself. If I was to live, I had to eat. I told myself that I had eaten worse. I took my bread and broke off a piece and followed the boy's example. I wondered if the weevils would grow in my stomach.

One bowl of soup and one biscuit was not enough to fill me, but that was all we were given. It didn't matter how big the boy was, the ration was the same. Any boy who didn't finish his small portion passed it to another. There wasn't a speck of food left on the tables when we finished our dinner.

I looked at the boys gathered around the tables. They had pale faces with hollowed eyes and gaps where teeth should be. But we were the lucky ones. As poor as the food was, we wouldn't starve to death in the workhouse. I thought of the hundreds of Irish outside the walls. Without food and shelter, how would they survive?

After dinner we went to the boys' yard. The barren yard was surrounded by tall stone walls. If one boy stood on top of another boy's shoulders, he couldn't reach the top of the wall. I felt like I was in a prison. I thought "what was my crime?"

I left the others and walked to the center of the yard and breathed. Fresh air filled my lungs. Out in the open, I could breathe deep and not gag on the stench of the workhouse. The wind brought me the scent of Ireland. I felt spring in the air and all that it promised. I closed my eyes and breathed. I tried to picture life beyond the walls; the greening of the valleys, water that tumbled over rocks in the streams, moonbeams on the fields.

Chapter 63

The dark came upon us. It was time to go inside. We walked to a narrow stairwell. The walls and steep steps were hard stone. It was so narrow that we could only walk single file. The light was dim. I pressed my hands against the opposing walls. My calves ached as I climbed each step.

Our sleeping area was a long, narrow room. There were no beds, but two wooden platforms that ran the length of each side of the room. On top of the platforms were filthy mattresses that were stuffed with straw. Each boy seemed to know where he was going as he walked down the hallway. I stumbled along not knowing where I should go. Fading light came through the high windows. Johnnie stood at the end of the hall beneath the last window. There was another open doorway behind him. He beckoned me forward.

I smiled. I don't why, but I had taken a liking to Johnnie. Some of the boys collapsed and lay down on the mattresses. Other boys sat on the edge of the long bed that they would all share. I weaved my way through them to Johnnie.

He eyed me as I approached and said, "You survived your first day."

"Are you surprised?"

"No, not at all." He motioned to the end of the platform. "If you want you can sleep here by me." He laughed. "I know you're cleaner than the rest of 'em."

I could see a hallway through the open door. I walked closer to Johnnie and felt a slight breeze on my face. He must have seen my puzzlement.

"What little fresh air we have," he nodded to the opening, "comes up the stairs. You'll breathe easier here and," he flicked his nose at the boys behind me, "the smell's not as bad."

I turned and looked at the room. Every inch of the platforms was taken. Some of the smaller boys curled at the top of the bed while other boys curled beneath them. The boys were squeezed so tight together that I couldn't tell where one body ended and another began.

Light faded from the windows. I was beyond tired. Johnnie lit a candle and placed it in a holder by the door. The room quieted. Boys talked in soft whispers. I went and laid on the bed next to the last boy on the platform. Johnnie sat on the edge of the bed next to me.

A door must have opened because a gust of air came into the room. The candle quivered.

A hushed cry came from the hallway. Other cries joined the first. Johnnie got up and took the candle. I don't know why, but I followed him.

Johnnie went into the hallway and walked to the door where the cries came from. I crept behind him. He raised the candle. The light illuminated another room just like ours.

I gasped.

Johnnie quickly turned and faced me.

I ignored his look of surprise and looked past him into the room that was filled with young boys. It was a pitiful sight to see. They were just children. They tried to muffle their cries when the light fell upon them. All I could think about was my little brother. Most of the boys were younger than Michael. If he stayed, he would be here with them. There were hundreds of boys squeezed together on the platforms. The littlest of the children seemed so sad. They were thin and fragile and frightened. I didn't understand why the children were alone. Some of their mothers like mine had to be here in the workhouse. Why weren't the little ones with their mothers?

Johnnie walked into the room with his candle. I waited in the doorway. He went to the wall sconce and lit its extinguished flame. The candle flickered and cast a soft glow in the darkness. The room hushed. The light seemed to bring comfort to the boys.

Johnnie walked back to me. He pushed me from the room.

CHAPTER 64

I laid down on our bed, but now I couldn't sleep. I closed my eyes and pictured the room filled with young boys.

I turned on my side to face Johnnie, who lay beside me. I asked, "Why can't they leave the poor children with their mothers?"

The candlelight glowed behind Johnnie. His jug ear cast a shadow across his dark cheek.

"Some of the boys were orphaned and some were abandoned."

I snapped, "What of the others?"

"I don't know," Johnnie sighed. "They separate the men and women because they don't want husbands sleeping with their wives. They don't want more Irish children." He turned onto his back and stared at the ceiling. "I don't why they won't let the little ones stay with their mothers."

The boy on the other side of me stirred. I knew I should be quiet and try to sleep like the others, but I couldn't.

I whispered, "Do you have family here?"

"I did."

I stared at his face and held my breath while I waited for him to go on.

"I can barely remember my Da. He went to England to work the harvest and never came back. We stayed with my

Grandma until she died. We had no money and no other family. We had no choice but to come here. This all happened before the potatoes turned black."

"How long have you been here?"

"I don't know. Four years, five years. It was so different when we came here. There was hardly anyone else in the workhouse. We had decent food at every meal. The room below us was a schoolroom. It wasn't filled with children like it is now."

I asked in disbelief, "there's another room of children downstairs?"

"One for boys and one for girls. There's a lot more children here than adults. That's why the older boys walk the wheel." He shifted and put his arm under his head for a pillow. "When I came here, they tried to teach us to read and write. I never took to it. I could see my Ma in the chapel on Sundays." His voice grew wistful. "The famine came and with it came the people who brought the sickness." I felt his body stiffen next to me. "One Sunday, my Ma wasn't in the chapel. I asked and asked about her until the Matron came and told me that my Ma died of the fever."

"I'm sorry."

"She's been gone a long time."

"But you still miss her?"

He turned away from me. I couldn't see his face. I put my hand gently on his shoulder and just let it rest there.

I tossed and turned all night. Boys cried out in their sleep. I don't know what nightmares haunted their dreams, but I thought how much worse can their dreams be than the life that they were living.

In the morning, one boy didn't have the strength to go to breakfast. They wouldn't let us carry him. We had no choice but to leave him. Johnnie said he would see that the boy was taken to the infirmary. It was a sad parting as the boys walked past and whispered their goodbyes to the boy they knew they would never see again.

CHAPTER 65

After breakfast we went to the jacks. There were two large buckets in our room that the boys used at night, but the buckets were only to pee in. You had to wait until morning to do your sit down.

There was a window high above the holes that were cut into the bench that was our toilet. Aidan climbed up on the bench. He grabbed ahold of the bottom of the windowsill and pulled himself up so that he could see outside.

One of the boys dropped his trousers and sat. He called up to Aidan, "Has the cart come out yet?"

"No, not yet," Aidan replied.

I climbed on top of the bench next to Aidan. I stretched. I wasn't tall enough to reach the windowsill so I jumped. My fingers grabbed hold and I pulled myself up. Aidan gave a look, but when he saw it was me, he nodded his OK.

I put my elbows on the sill like Aidan had and pressed my face against the glass. From our high perch we saw over the wall that surrounded the workhouse. We saw the river and the road that ran next to the workhouse.

"The buildings are in the way. You can't see the back gate from here," Aidan said. "That's where the cart will come from."

The boy below us said, "It must have been a bad night if the cart hasn't come out yet."

He no sooner said the words before I saw the cart come round the back wall. It was a second before I understood what my eyes saw.

"Good Lord have mercy," I said.

The cart was filled with bodies. There were no coffins. The poor were not even wrapped in sheets. Their only coverings were the clothes they wore in the sick house. I swallowed the bile that came up my throat.

"How many are there?" I asked.

"It's hard to say," Aidan said. "Maybe 20. We can't see how many bodies are hidden by the wooden sides of the cart."

"Where are they taking them?"

Aidan looked down at the boy. "You tell them, Matthew. You're the one who saw it."

The boy had pulled up his pants and now stood below us.

"There're taking the bodies to the graveyard at Abbeystrewry. They dug a pit next to the abandoned church. When they get to the pit they'll just toss them in."

I shouted, "It can't be true."

"I saw them throw the bodies from the cart with my own eyes when we were on our way to the workhouse."

"Tell him what you heard, Matthew," Aidan said.

Matthew sat on the edge of the bench and stared at his hands in his lap. "I heard a voice moan from down in the pit. I knew that someone still had to be alive." He rubbed his small hands up and down his thighs. "The men either didn't hear the cries or didn't care. They just kept tossing the bodies."

My elbow slipped. Aidan caught me before I fell. He helped me back up to the windowsill. I looked in his eyes and said, "It can't be true."

"But it is. Look at the cart. There's no place left at the workhouse to bury the dead. Every morning the cart leaves with those who died during the night. Every afternoon it comes back empty."

I stared at the dead on the cart. I pictured myself among them. My stomach cramped. I pushed back and slid down the wall to the bench. I jumped to the floor. I felt my stomach spasm. I dropped my trousers and sat down just in time.

CHAPTER 66

Sometimes all it took was just a cough in the night. When morning came, the boy who coughed would be too weak to get out of bed. They'd take the boy to the sickroom and then one of the hundreds of boys who lingered outside the workhouse gates would be let in to take the sick boy's place.

My days settled into a familiar routine. We woke at the same time, went to eat our meager meals at the same time, went to bed at the same time, and of course spent our dreaded walk at the wheel at the same time.

In the room with the wheel, I had to escape the constant monotonous drudgery. I stared out the high windows as I pushed and walked. I let the outside weather form the dreams in my mind. If there was bright sunshine, I'd picture a walk through the green fields on a hill by my home. If it was dark and cloudy, I'd walk along the shore by the ocean and try to feel the rain on my face. I wouldn't let my family come into my daydreams. I couldn't bear the sadness of not being with them.

I'd walk next to Aidan as we pushed the wheel. Sometimes he'd give me a strange look and I'd wonder if I talked aloud in my daydreams.

The change came slowly in our steps as Aidan and I walked the endless circle. I thought the difference was that I was getting stronger until the day came when I realized that my friend was getting weaker. It was a hard thing to know.

The meager portion of food that they gave us might be enough to sustain a boy, but it wasn't enough for a growing young man.

Chapter 67

On Sundays a priest would come from St. Patrick's Cathedral in Skibbereen to say Mass. We had no choice. All the boys went to the chapel together. They made us sit quietly, but they couldn't stop the younger boys from their constant fidgeting.

I tried to be one of the first in line as we walked off to the chapel. The women had their Mass before us. I hoped that I could catch a glimpse of my Ma and sisters as they left the chapel, but so far I hadn't seen them.

It'd been weeks since we came to the workhouse. I was deeply worried about my family. My nights had been haunted ever since the day I saw the cart full of the dead leave the back of the workhouse. I worried so because I knew every day another cart was carrying the dead away. I prayed for my family and especially my Ma. The last time I saw her she seemed so weak and fragile.

Johnnie said at the beginning of the famine, the priest was given the names of those who had died in the sickroom during the past week. He read the names at Mass so that the boys could pray for the souls of the departed. What the priest didn't know was that we never were told if our parents had died. A boy would sit in the chapel for Sunday Mass and learn from the mouth of the priest that his mother or father, sister or brother had died. Johnnie said it was terrible. The boys who learned they lost a loved one collapsed with grief. They wailed. They sobbed.

Boys began to dread going to the chapel. When the reading of the list began, the boys covered their ears so that they couldn't hear the names. They didn't want to know that their parents had died.

The priest stopped reading the list because the boys became too distraught. Now, without the reading of the list, there was no way for us to know if our loved ones were alive or dead.

I became obsessed with knowing if my Ma and sisters were OK. I asked Johnnie to check on my family. He was able to go where the rest of us couldn't. If anyone could find out about my family, it was Johnnie.

I pestered and pestered Johnnie until I finally got my wish.

It was a Sunday afternoon. Sunday was the only day of the week when we didn't have to walk the wheel. They let us spend the afternoon in the boys' yard. It was a glorious spring day. There wasn't a cloud in the sky. I saw the tops of the trees in bloom above the workhouse walls. I could hear the birds as they danced above the budding green leaves that swayed with the warn breeze. It was the kind of day that gave me hope.

Johnnie snuck up behind me and said in a low voice that only I could hear, "We have to be quick. There isn't much time."

I turned, but he was already gone. I saw him weave his way through the boys in the yard. I followed. He waited for me inside the doorway. I could tell by his face that something was wrong.

"What?" I asked.

He twisted his lips like he was trying to gather his courage to talk.

I waited, but he just shook and then lowered his head. He turned and walked down the hallway.

CHAPTER 68

Johnnie led me to the chapel. The candles still burned from the last Mass. The chapel was empty and quiet except for two women who stood behind the pews. They wore long dresses and white bonnets. Johnnie stayed by the doorway. He motioned me forward.

I walked slowly and tentatively toward the women. The smaller of the two raised her hand to her mouth and stifled a cry.

"Danny," the taller one said and stepped closer.

I couldn't believe my eyes. Mary and Joanna were alive and well. I moved quickly and hugged my oldest sister. Joanna joined us. They cried, which brought tears to my eyes. I stepped back. I just wanted to take in the sight of them.

"Look at your clothes," I said.

Mary seemed embarrassed. She said, "They gave us these clothes for our journey."

Joanna lifted her skirt. "We have shoes too."

"Your journey?"

Joanna looked to her older sister to answer.

"You don't know?"

"Know what?"

Mary took a breath and swallowed. "They've picked some of the orphan girls to go to Australia. They don't have enough women there. They need women to do the housework. They gave us these clean clothes." She smoothed her dress. "And paid for our passage. We're to work when we get there to pay them back." She took Joanna's hand. "They'll let us go together because we're sisters."

It was too much all at once. I stepped back and shook my head. Something she said wasn't right. Suddenly, my heart tightened.

"Where's Ma?"

Mary's face turned into a mask of sadness. She said in a soft voice, "You don't know."

I sprang forward and shook her. "Where's Ma?"

"She died two nights after we got here." Mary took my hands from her arms and held them. She said as if her words could comfort me, "She wasn't alone." She looked at Joanna. "Ma slept between us. She went to sleep and didn't wake up."

I screamed, "No!"

Mary held me tight against her chest and said, "Ma prayed for you before she fell asleep."

I crumbled. I felt something die within me. Only Mary's hands held me up.

I heard a voice behind me. "We've got to go. Now."

Johnnie took my arm and pulled me from Mary. I heard Joanna crying my name as Johnnie dragged me from the chapel.

That was the last time I saw my sisters.

CHAPTER 69

A numbness came over me. I can't explain how it felt. Johnnie wouldn't leave me. Wherever I went, he went with me. The other boys stayed away. I went through the motions of living. I ate what was put in front of me and walked the endless wheel.

Days passed. During the night my Ma came to me in my dreams. We'd sing in the kitchen as she made my breakfast. She was young and happy and healthy and beautiful. I'd wake to the gloom of the room. To the thin, hollow faces of the other abandoned boys.

Aidan's steps grew weaker as we pushed the wheel. I knew it was just a matter of time. Boys didn't thrive in the workhouse. I tried to take some of his burden, but I hadn't the strength. He'd wheeze as he walked. His face was pale beneath his red peach fuzz. The cough came. It worsened through the week. The cough racked his chest and doubled him over across the spar that we pushed. The morning came when he was too weak to get up from our bed. I thought, "When the strongest can't survive, what chance did the rest of us have?"

He was my friend and I owed him a goodbye, but I couldn't. I just couldn't. Numbness enveloped me. I walked by Aidan without a word of farewell. I went and got my breakfast.

I couldn't sleep. I dreaded the night as much as I dreaded the coming day. I knew I would die in the workhouse. I came here for my Ma and sisters and now that they were gone there was no reason for me to stay.

Johnnie stirred beside me. I knew he was awake. I turned on my side. I couldn't see his face because the candlelight was behind him. He put his hand on my arm. I breathed. I took and held his hand.

"Will they stop me if I try to leave," I whispered.

He took a long time to answer and then he said, "They lock the gate to keep people out, not to keep people in. We're not prisoners. They won't stop you. But why would you leave? You'd die out there."

"I'll die in here."

"I can get you some extra bread. I'll sneak it from the kitchen in my pockets. You can eat it at night while the others are asleep."

"Come with me."

He pulled his hand away. He turned on his back. I watched the rise and fall of his chest. Somewhere in the room, a boy cried out in his dreams.

"I can't," Johnnie sighed. "I have a life here. I have food and a place to sleep."

"I know how to find food. It's summer, we'll sleep outside."

"And what will you do when winter comes?"

"I can't stay here, Johnnie."

"Then go," he said harshly and covered his face with his arm.

I pulled his arm from his face. Tears coated his cheek.

His voice quivered as he said, "I can't go with you, Danny. I'm too scared."

I held his hand. I wanted to wipe the tears from his cheek. There were no words that I could offer to take away his fear.

"I have to go."

He rolled and turned his back to me.

CHAPTER 70

As soon as there was enough feeble light, I quietly got out of bed. Johnnie lay with his arm over his face. I walked and leaned over him and quietly said, "I'm sorry."

He lowered his arm and our eyes met.

"I wish I was brave like you," he said.

"I'm not brave. I'd rather starve than stay here."

"I wish you wouldn't go."

"I know."

"You are my friend."

"And you're mine."

His eyes teared. I don't know why I did it, but I leaned over and kissed his forehead just like my mother used to kiss me goodnight.

I took nothing with me. There was nothing to take. The world was eerily quiet. The porter was at the gatehouse. He stood and stared out at the road beyond the gate. I startled him when I came up behind him. He turned and gave me a mean glare.

"What do you want?" he asked.

"I want to leave."

He studied me and then finally said, "If I let you out, I'll not let you back in."

"Just let me go."

He angrily snatched the keys from his belt and unlocked the gate. He opened the gate just far enough for me to squeeze through. He quickly locked the gate behind me.

"Don't come crawling back. It'll do you no good."

I ignored him and walked down the road in the twilight that came before dawn. Dark shapes stirred on the hillside as I walked by. The shapes took human form as some of the homeless slowly sat up. Others seemed too weak to rise. Some were so still, I wondered if they were still alive. I don't know how many people there were, but there had to be hundreds. I put my hand over my mouth, but I couldn't escape the smell of human waste and filth. I stayed on the road as I walked away from the workhouse.

The road from the front gate led to the road that went around the side of the workhouse. I sat on the hillside where the two roads merged. I was away from the stench of the homeless that gathered around the gates of the workhouse. The sun rose and warmed me. I sat and waited for the cart that brought out the dead.

CHAPTER 71

The cart came around the bend of the road that led from the back gate of the workhouse. The horse struggled as it drew the heavy cart slowly forward. I sat still and stared. The cart came closer and I could see the faces of the dead. The bodies were piled one on top of another. The old lay with the young and the men now lay atop the women they were denied to be with in the workhouse. I got up and followed the cart.

It was a slow journey. The cart groaned under the heavy weight of the dead. I followed with my head down and my hands folded.

When we got to Abbeystrewry, I stopped and waited by the ruins of the old church. I could see the pit that Matthew talked about from where I stood. I was too afraid to go any closer. I stood and watched from afar.

Two men waited with shovels on their shoulders. They stopped the cart near the gaping hole. The men dropped their shovels and walked to the back of the cart. One man grabbed the arms and the other the feet of a dead woman. The swung the body together in a well-practiced rhythm and tossed the woman into the air. The body landed with a hollow thump. I pictured my Ma. I didn't realize I bit my lip until I tasted blood.

It took only minutes to empty the cart. The men took their shovels and tossed dirt atop the bodies. Their job finished, they shouldered their shovels and walked away. Now, free of its heavy burden, the horse pulled the cart back toward the workhouse.

Matthew's story was true.

I realized that my Ma had no priest to give her the final blessing. There was no individual grave or marker to show my Ma's final resting place. My chest tightened. I forced one foot forward and then the other. I looked down at my feet as I walked toward the pit.

I could see the outline of the bodies beneath the dirt. I slowly raised my eyes. The earth mounds seemed to stretch forever. Somewhere in front of me, my Ma lay among the thousands in the field of the dead.

I dropped to my knees by the edge of the pit. I folded my hands and prayed for my Ma.

CHAPTER 72

"Danny."

I thought I must be dreaming. I heard my name called again, but this time the voice was closer.

"Danny."

The call didn't come from the pit, it came from behind me. A fiddle was placed on the ground by my knees. Two hands helped me to my feet and slowly turned me.

"It is you," said Uncle Seamus.

He took off my cap and studied me carefully. His eyes were filled with sadness.

"I don't know if it is luck that I found you or if it is God's will." He set the cap back on my head. "I went to your cottage that's no longer there. I went to the Sheriff and he said you were at the workhouse. When I got to the workhouse, they said you left this morning. And now, I've finally found you, one living boy here among the dead."

He motioned to the grave. "Your family?"

I said in a voice not more than whisper, "My Ma."

"And your sisters?"

I shook my head. "No, they're not here. They're gone to Australia."

He bent and picked up his fiddle. He curled his hand around my shoulder and led me away from my Ma's grave.

He must have known I needed time to myself. We walked in silence. I'd catch him staring at me out of the corner of his eye. We stopped at a pub at the crossroads. It was mid-afternoon, so the pub was not busy. He set his fiddle on the table. There was food to be had if you had money. He ordered tea for me and whiskey for him. When the drinks came he downed the whiskey and held the glass out for another. He ordered a bowl of stew for me. The stew was warm from the fire. I broke apart the bread and dunked it in the stew. I had forgotten the taste of meat. I chewed slowly and savored the flavor. Uncle Seamus just sat and watched as I ate.

He asked if I wanted another bowl, but my stomach was full so I just shook my head. He pulled his pipe from his pocket and lit it. The rising smoke matched the color of his hair. He reached into his pocket and pulled out an envelope.

"This is why I came to find you. Caitlin sent it to me. It's for you."

He set the envelope on the table between us.

I stared at the smudged, winkled envelope. He pushed it closer. I lifted and slowly opened the envelope. There were two white pages of writing and something else. I knew it was paper money, but I didn't know what it was worth. I stared at the pages. I recognized names and some of the words. I smoothed the pages on the table and traced the lines with my finger. It was hopeless.

"I can't read this."

"You don't have to. The money will get you to America. There you can learn how to read the letter."

CHAPTER 73

"We should be off," Uncle Seamus said. He stared at me once again with that look of concern in his eyes.

My mind had wandered, I'm not sure where it went or for how long. The letter was still on the table before me. I carefully folded it and put it in my pocket.

We left the pub and started down the lane. I felt like I was in a dream. My life had suddenly changed and I didn't know how to change with it.

I asked, "Am I really to go to America?"

Uncle Seamus laughed. "You are, Danny. We'll have to find a boat for your crossing. You'll be there before the winter storms."

I slid my hand in my pocket and wrapped my fingers around the letter.

We came to the crossroads. I stopped and looked down the familiar road that led to my village. I knew I couldn't leave without saying my goodbye.

"I need to visit my Da's grave," I said to Uncle Seamus.

I expected him to argue, but he just nodded. Together, we walked down the road of my childhood.

The fields were in summer bloom. The sky was a startling blue with just a wisp of clouds. I tried to capture every image to make a picture in my mind, to make a memory that I could take with me. Uncle Seamus didn't rush me. It was like he knew what I was doing.

We walked up the hill that led to Carrigillihy. When we got to the top, I looked to the valley below. I stood dumbstruck. My village was gone. I knew that the landlord had tumbled some cottages, but I didn't know he had destroyed the whole village.

We walked down the hill. I felt like I had walked from one cemetery to another. Abbeystrewry was the cemetery for the Irish dead. Carrigillihy was the cemetery for the Irish who were driven from their homes. The tumbled stone walls were all that remained to mark the passage of the countless generations of Irish who lived on the land.

I walked by the cabins and stared at the ruins. Each cottage brought back a memory. I knew every family who had lived in our clachan. I wondered how many were buried under the rubble, how many were in the workhouse, how many were homeless? I knew few if any had gone to America. We were too poor of a village.

I wondered how many Irish villages like mine had disappeared.

Across the valley, I could see the Manor House. The stone wall was finished. The fields that surrounded the Manor House were not filled with Irish who tended their potatoes. The fields were filled with cows.

CHAPTER 74

As I walked down the lane to my cottage, I tried to remember the happy times before our world had changed. I looked to the hilltop where Paddy and Caitlin hoped to build their cottage and raise a family. The hilltop that Michael and I somersaulted down. We rose laughing and so dizzy that our heads spun.

While they weeded the potatoes, my sisters would talk and laugh as only girls could. I'd hear my Ma sing from the kitchen as she boiled our dinner.

Memories were all that remained of my cottage. Grass had grown over the thatch and ivy twisted around the stones.

I slowly walked the field to my Da's grave. He rested beside his father. I don't know how many of our generations lay in the earth beside them. I kneeled and tried to say a prayer, but the words wouldn't come. Uncle Seamus took his fiddle to his chin and played. He played the *Minstrel Boy.* I sank back on my heels. I put my hand on my Da's grave. I could see his face. I'd never know another man as strong or as brave as my Da.

I don't know why the tears started or where they came from. I cried. My cries turned to sobs. My chest hurt. I couldn't breathe. I knew the sobs were not just for my Da.

Uncle Seamus stopped his playing and sat beside me. He wrapped his arm around my shoulder and held me tight against his chest.

I couldn't stop sobbing.

"It's OK, Danny. It's OK."

I tried to stop, but I couldn't. I tried to draw a breath, but the air wouldn't come into my lungs. My chest felt like it was on fire. I had to find a way to let go of all the pain that I carried. Uncle Seamus rocked me like I was a baby. "It's OK, Danny. It'll pass."

I don't know how long Uncle Seamus held and rocked me. I don't know how long it was until I could breathe. My sobs turned to tears and then to teardrops.

The pain has never left me.

CHAPTER 75

I don't know where the day went. Evening was upon us. We left my Da's grave and walked back to my cottage. The hearth was all that remained. Uncle Seamus searched beneath the rubble around the hearth and found some peat. He made a fire in the remains of our fireplace.

"I'll be back," I said.

Uncle Seamus gave me his look of concern.

I shrugged it off and walked away. My chest still hurt, but at least I could breathe. It was a short walk across the field to the berry patch. Never had I seen so many berries in the patch. No one was left to pick them. I'd eat one and toss one in my cap. When my cap was full I carried it back to Uncle Seamus.

I gave him my cap. He nodded his thanks and sat by the fire.

The clouds rolled in and brought the darkness. I sat close by the fire with Uncle Seamus. There would be no stars tonight. I peered into the blackness. I shivered with my fear of the dark, my fear of goblins and banshees and the famine dead that walked at night.

Uncle Seamus finished the berries and tossed me my cap. He took a silver flask from his pocket. He took a sip and then slid the flask back into his coat. He stared intently at the fire.

Minutes passed in silence. I wondered what he saw.

He picked up a cut of peat. He broke off a piece and tossed it into the fire.

He sighed and said, "I fear the blight is a terrible blessing." A chill came with his words. I tightened my coat. I shoved my hands into my pockets. I curled my fingers around the envelope.

He stared at me and said, "The blight has killed the weakest and is driving the strongest of us away." He held my gaze. "Our future lies with you and the Irish in America." He tossed the rest of the peat into the fire.

As a child, I didn't understand his words.

CHAPTER 76

I awoke to voices.

"There's no harm done. We just stopped for the night."

I recognized Uncle Seamus' voice. I came down from the clouds of sleep. I opened my eyes and beheld the devil. My body tensed. I slowly stood. Morning dew covered the grass. The black steed pawed the earth and snorted.

Coghlan sat on his horse. He didn't pay me no mind.

Uncle Seamus bent and picked up his fiddle. "The boy and I will be on our way."

Coghlan noticed me standing. It took him a few seconds to recognize who I was. His face and voice hardened.

"Why aren't you in the workhouse?"

"The boy's with me," Uncle Seamus said.

Coghlan snapped, "What's he to you?"

"He's family. My niece is married to his brother. He just wanted to stop and say goodbye to his Da. We'll be going now."

I could feel Coghlan's hatred in the look that passed between us. His eyes burned with anger. He knew I knew the evil in him. His hand went into his coat. If I had a gun, I would've killed him.

Uncle Seamus held his hand up in a pacifying gesture. "We'll go."

Coghlan's hand stayed in his coat. Uncle Seamus walked toward me with his back to the horseman. I met Coghlan's stare. I wouldn't look away. I waited for him to draw the pistol.

Uncle Seamus walked in front of me and said, "Come on, Danny."

He blocked my view of Coghlan. I moved to the side, but the moment had passed. Coghlan sat back on his horse. His hand came out empty. He grabbed both reins.

I drew a breath.

"Don't ever come back here," Coghlan said. He wheeled his horse and rode off.

I walked away from Uncle Seamus and peed on the ground. My hands shook as I held myself.

We walked down our narrow lane to the main road that would take us to the ships. We went through Carrigillihy, the village that was no more. I was still seething. I picked up a stone and threw it as far as I could.

"We can't win, Danny. We've worn their chains for 700 years. We'll not break them now."

"It's not right." I felt the sadness come upon me, but I shook it off. I let my anger drive the sadness away. "They've taken my family. They've taken my home. They've taken my village." I stopped and looked at Uncle Seamus and asked, "Why didn't we fight?"

"For seven centuries we fought. Men with pikes can't win against men who have cannons."

I wanted to hit something, anything, but there was nothing left to hit.

"Take your anger with you, Danny. Take it to America. Never forget what you lived through and never forget who took our food when we were starving. Never forget how you feel right now. Tell your story to anyone who will listen. Our fight will never be won here without the help of our Irish in America."

CHAPTER 77

"It's the Liberty, Danny. It's a fine ship. It took Caitlin and Paddy safe to America and the Good Lord willing, it'll take you too."

We stood on the wharf. I remembered the ship. How many years ago was it that I stood at the same spot and said my good-byes to Paddy? I never thought I'd see him again, but now I thought I might. The ship was all hustle and bustle.

"Come on. I hope it's not too late." Uncle Seamus quickly walked to and then up the gangway. He darted around seamen who carried provisions to the hold.

I followed as best as I could. Everything was new and exciting. It was an adventure. The masts and riggings towered over me and the wooden boards swayed beneath my feet. No one stopped Uncle Seamus as he made his way to the rear of the ship. A tall man stood on the quarterdeck. He was dressed in a hat and a fine coat. One of the coat sleeves was empty. Uncle Seamus stopped and waited until the Captain beckoned him forward. Uncle Seamus motioned for me to stay.

The Captain smiled and said, "Over that last drink, I thought you told me that you'd never leave dear old Ireland."

"And I won't," replied Uncle Seamus. "But Captain Sanford, I've got a young man who needs to go and you need to take him." He motioned me to join them.

"My ship's full."

Uncle Seamus put his hand on my shoulder. "This is, Danny. You took his older brother Paddy and my niece Caitlin to America. Now Danny needs to join them. They sent money for his crossing."

Uncle Seamus tapped my pocket. I took out the envelope.

"You're Paddy's younger brother?" The Captain looked at me with interest. He stepped forward and searched my face. I could smell his tobacco. His eyes were the color of morning fog.

"He is," Uncle Seamus said.

"I owe your brother a debt. Keep your money. When you see Paddy tell him the debt is paid." He shouted, "Tommy."

A sailor ran up onto the quarterdeck. He was small and scruffy, but wiry. He wore a red knit cap that was as frayed as his clothes.

"We'll have a cabin boy for this crossing. He'll bunk with the crew. He looks half-starved. Take him down to the galley and get him something to eat."

Tommy looked down his nose at me as if he couldn't be bothered.

"His brother brought you luck. Maybe the boy will do the same."

"What's your brother's name?" Tommy asked.

"It's Paddy."

Tommy turned from me to the Captain with a questioning stare on his face. The Captain nodded.

Tommy looked at me anew and said, "Come on. We'll get you something to eat."

CHAPTER 78

We left with the morning tide. It was a cloudy, drizzly day. The Irish came up from the hold and stood at the rail to catch their last glimpse of the country that gave them birth. I stood by Captain Sanford on the quarterdeck. My heart felt like it was being torn in two. I didn't want to leave, but I knew I had to go.

The wind brought us the music. Uncle Seamus stood on the wharf with his fiddle. He played the *Minstrel Boy*, the song of parting, the song that always made my Da cry.

Gigi sighed. She gently caressed the petals of the Irish Easter lilies.

"What happened to Danny?" Caitlin asked.

"He came to Garryowen, but he didn't stay. My Grandmother said that Danny carried the pain of Ireland inside him. He traveled from city to city and told his story of the Great Hunger to anyone who would listen. Rumors said he fell in with the Fenians. Other rumors said he went back to Ireland. We don't know. For us he just disappeared."

"And Michael?" Caitlin asked.

Michael's life was a gift from Danny. His story's best saved for another day.

AUTHOR'S NOTE

Ireland was one of the most populous countries in Europe in 1845. There were over 8 million Irish at the start of the Potato Famine. One million Irish would die during the time of the Great Hunger. The potato famine also set in motion the great emigration of the Irish to America. By the time Ireland achieved independence in 1921 the population was less than 4 million. According to the 2010 United States Census, there are over 34 million Americans who claim Irish heritage.

The Minstrel Boy was written by Thomas Moore. It is widely believed that Moore composed the song in remembrance of his friends who were killed in the Irish Rebellion of 1798.

I am indebted to Sister Mary Angela Feeney, P.B.V.M. and Patrick L. Coleman who helped inspire this story. They gathered the history of my mother's ancestors in their book *At Grandpa's Knee.*

My Grandmother lived to be almost 100 years old. Her stories of my Irish heritage will always live within me.

My wife and children and grandchildren are my daily reminder of the Irish's love of family.